Old Friends

- An Anthology

by Kings' School

Al Barsha -

Cover created by

Bissan Kadi

Kings' School Al Barsha

Young Author Academy FZCO
Dubai, United Arab Emirates

www.youngauthoracademy.com

ISBN: 9798398699609

Printed by Amazon Direct Publishing.

Contents

Kings' School Al Barsha

Stories

by

- Year Three -

Zoya Norat

Arhaan Shah

Neil Ratan Lahoti

Ahmed Nabil Salim

The Galactic Adventure of ZAINA

by Zoya Norat

In a world full of wonder, sitting in her room, was an adventurous girl called Zaina who was looking though her telescope wondering how cool it would be to be an astronaut.

Her big opportunity would come tomorrow when she would go to space. She was so excited she couldn't sleep. Daydreaming of how it would be like because she was obsessed with space.

The next morning was take-off day. As her parents drove her to the rocket, she drew pictures of planets, not listening to a single word they were saying.

She was going to be the first nine-year-old to set foot in space. The car approached the rocket station and there was a sea of people waiting to see the amazing Zaina. She was nervous and excited.

The space team took her to the rocket with her parents beside her ready to say their goodbyes. Although she had months of training, she couldn't believe what was happening, and she was still a little scared. She hugged her parents goodbye before she took her first step in the rocket with a big smile on her face.

Zogalog

Not long after, she finally took off. The rocket was shaking as it went off to space at the speed of light. The rocket shook even more and the space team ejected out of the rocket. The rocket went faster and faster until it crashed and landed on an unknown planet.

The planet was an ombre blue purple and pink colour. There were two sides: a dark side and a blue side. She was a little scared.

She saw a blue light she followed it and there was a giant sapphire. Beside it, there was an alien who had followed the blue light as well.

Zaina saw the cute little fluffy creature which was a rosé gold colour. He said his name was Yetemi. Yetemi welcomed her to Zogolog. He explained that the sapphire only is revealed to a strong and very brave person and it was Zaina. The little alien introduced her to all its friends. They were all very friendly and very welcoming. Then Yetemi, the little alien, told her that the other side was the bad side but the good side wanted the bad side to go away so they thought of a plan. They were going to have a battle and try to win, and agree that the dark side aliens must move away.

Zocalo

So they demanded the dark side to have a battle because Zaina wanted to go home but the good rocket was on the bad side. They have battles by playing a game like cricket but they call it Zocalo. The good side always lost because they were short and slow and their only power is cuteness. The sapphire gave you super powers which was super speed and strength. The Aliens on the bad side were a shimmering blue and black. They had long legs and were very fast, and very good at zocalo.

The Big Battle of Zocalo

The battle was about to begin with a big drum. When the drum was first heard, the battle would begin. Soon the drum was heard. As the drum played, the aliens got ready to start the battle.

Zaina was scared but she had faith in herself. They had started Zocalo. She was so fast that every thing seemed like it was in slow motion. She was a fielder and got the meteor a million times. So they won the zocalo game. Then Zaina declared that they all be friends, so the sapphire lifted the darkness from the dark side. Zaina finally got to see the beauty of the planet and was ready to go home.

Arrival Home

Yetemi and his family escorted her to the rocket and took her safely back to her house on earth. When Zaina landed, she saw the space team were all safe. And when she saw her mum, she gave her the biggest hug in the world. Before Yetemi left, he gifted her the sapphire.

The BFF's

by Arhaan Shah

They had always been together, for as long as they could remember. They had always been the best of friends. They had taught each other everything they knew, relentlessly preparing them for life in the outside world (their parents were very protective, so they were home-schooled). This was the moment they'd both been waiting for; their first sleepover.

It all started one night, when the friends were having a sleepover, the ground shook and rumbled the country; back and forth, back and forth. The friends woke up in shock and fear. They ran as fast as their little legs could take them to Isabella's parents'.

Elizabeth, Isabella and her parents ran out of the house! They called the police and ran to their car, they drove full speed to the ocean, and took inflatable lifeboats out of the car, put the lifeboats in the ocean and jumped in.

The whole neighborhood was a zoo and everyone was screaming, running and all of them were thinking the same thing; what is going on right now? There were only two lifeboats, so Isabella and her family were in one lifeboat and Elizabeth and Rexy (her poodle, who was also enjoying the sleepover) in another. Isabella felt bad for leaving Elizabeth alone, so she started crying for her friend. Luckily, there was a small island nearby, so the people on both lifeboats paddled to the shore of the island.

When they reached, Isabella was so relieved to see her friend again, that she hugged Elizabeth so tight as if to never leave her again.

They built a small hut, and over the days, they learnt how to survive in the wild. For two weeks, they stayed at the island. They made a bed from leaves, a pillow from leaves and wood, a house from mud, bark, and sand, food from meat and the fruit on the palm trees, and water from filtered seawater. But life on the Island was harsh and it was getting difficult to survive.

One day, they saw a ship passing by their tiny hut. When Elizabeth saw the ship, an idea formed inside her mind like a pot made from clay! As fast as a cheetah, Elizabeth ran to Isabella and her parents and told them the plan. After that, all of them got to work.

Isabella wrote 'SOS' as large as she could. Her parents made a tower from wood so tall that the people on the top deck of the ship should see it, and Elizabeth started shouting, "Please save us"!

After Isabella and her parents finished their job, they all joined in. Eventually, the ship turned their attention towards them. The captain of the ship said, "OK, we'll save you."

At last, Isabella's parents and her friend screamed with delight. They climbed aboard the ship and told the captain the location of their house. After a while, Elizabeth, Rex, Isabella and her parents returned to their homes, and Elizabeth told her her parent's about her journey.

Adventures of Jack and Kevin

by Neil Ratan Lahoti

Chapters:

1.   What's That?

"Look! Look down there!" His voice could just be heard above the sound of the aeroplane's engine and the shrieking wind in the ears.

"Can you see it?"

"Huh? I can't see anything."

The names were Jack and Kevin. They were best friends and were always together in ANY case. Actually, any! You name it.

"Do you think we are brave enough to jump out of the plane?" Jack said.

"Of course!" Kevin replied, "How can we never? Let's jump in three, two, one... GO!"

2. Where Are We?

Sadly, there was nothing special to be seen from the area they landed in. But they were in the ocean and took no damage. Luckily though, in their bags there was a compass and it said they were facing South-West. So they simply turned North, and started swimming. And swimming. And swimming.

After about an hour, they found a tropical island. They rested for a while under a coconut tree and they drank and ate sweet, delicious coconut water.

Kevin then saw something and called Jack, "Do you see that thing there? It looks like a shipwreck... See it?"

"No... take me?" Jack said.

"Fine, I hope we find treasure!" Kevin said.

So they headed to the ship and went inside. As easy as that. No problems, straight inside the ship. They found treasure. It sounds like a stunning miracle but Kevin and Jack treated it like just a last-minute find. They put some treasure in the bags to save for later. But, ATTACK! A few people started running at them. They quickly hid.

Jack said it. "We need to get out of here mate! No more messing round. Let's get to work!"

So they gathered supplies, such as wood, leaves and food (coconuts and fish). They also used the webs the spiders had created and used it as string. So then they created a beautiful, stable raft and set sail North.

3.   A Break in Cuba

After a tiring day, they finally reached land. They discovered they were in Cuba, because there was a Cuban flag on the shore. So they planned on asking one of the friendly, kind locals if they can refreshen and restock their energy in their huts. So they spent half an hour finding a person's house to stay in.

Finally, they found a kind man named Adam. So they stayed there for a day, chit-chatting, sleeping and watching TV. Jack then said, "I don't want to stay in Cuba! I want to go to North America. Better in the continents!"

So Kevin said, "Same for me, but how get there? I am not going on another boat. I'll fall seasick!"

So Jack said, "Hmmm. I've got an idea. But it's cheeky! He went over to Kevin and whispered it. They were in action.

4.   At the Airport

So when they reached the airport with Adam's car, they entered and WOW. It was bustling, with all queues full, people eating to their hearts content, and even securities restricting entries! So they quietly tiptoed behind two people's backs, to where the check in to Mexico was. It took ages for their turn, but eventually the lady was talking.

When they were done, they entered the toughest part of all. Security. If they got caught, they could be arrested. So Jack whispered to Kevin real quiet. "Fast or slow and quiet?"

Kevin replied, "Slow and quiet."

Their teamwork was improving, so they tiptoed around the corners, sprinted through the scanners and hopped onto the elevator. They did it! But they needed a boarding pass so they could hop on to the plane. So they used their previous plan, to sneak behind people. Let's fast forward, probably a few minutes, and they were on the plane and voila! Off they went to Mexico!

5.   In Mexico

After a memorable flight, when they were greeted by other flight attendants and were led to the exit.

After catching a taxi and paying with some of the treasure, they went to Chichén Itzá for touring.

It was beautiful, but then some people came over. They asked, "You guys seem to be having fun. Where are your parents?"

Jack and Kevin frowned. They replied, "We are orphans. We are all educated and having a nice life. We are looking for a home."

The people got sad. They didn't want two homeless kids roaming around in Chichén Itzá! They wanted two happy kids in a stunning house.

The lady made her decision, and gave them a hotel to stay in. She said, "Have a nice day in

Mexico. Bye!"

So the kids went to the hotel and played board games that they had in their bags, they had triple tasty snacks, and then slept. They were having a great day but when they left the hotel, there was a problem...

6. Oh no!

As soon as the kids left the hotel to explore Mexico, they saw a lot of homeless people sitting next to the walls of huge buildings with a jar in front of them, with a few coins in them worth a Centavo. Jack and Kevin decided they should give, not ignore. So they gave some of the treasure and gold they had found at the island and even offered them to stay in their room! So they agreed, and then they were having LOADS of fun. Eating delicious food, swimming, and chit-chatting!

7.   One Small Change, One Big Difference!

After that small act of kindness, that homeless person got the opportunity to buy a home. And he did. After that day, Kevin, Jack and the homeless person (which they found out was named Gill) had a very great life ahead of him.

8.   Who's That?

One day, when they were strolling around in town, they bumped into a person. Just like almost everyone has done. Like many people, they just take a look at the other person, and then just leave. But that didn't happen. They looked at each other, and immediately felt familiar with each other somehow. Jack and Kevin looked at him, he looked at them. Both people were silent until Jack asked, "What's your name?"

He replied, "James." James thought, what a

decent start!"

Then they started really 'talking' and were really understanding each other.

9. A New Friend!

They became soooo happy, Kevin invited James to the hotel, the hotel he and Jack were staying at. James sounded great with the plan, so they went to the room and talked. And talked. And TALKED, about old friends, food, recent doings and more!

AFTER that, they introduced James to Gill and Gill to James, then they lived Happily Ever After in Mexico.

Friends In Need Are Friends Indeed

by Ahmed Nabil Salim

"Look! Look down there!" His voice could just about be heard above the sound of the airplane's engine and the shrieking wind in their ears.

"Can you see it?"

"I can see a flock of beautiful birds," said Jack nervously.

"But look behind the birds, can't you see the long metal bar peeping out into the clouds?" pointed Ali.

"Oh yes! Now I can see it, Is it the tallest building of the world?" inquired Jack.

"Hurrah! Indeed, it is! It means that we have reached Dubai," exclaimed Ali.

It all began when the two boys started their journey from London to Dubai. Jack and Ali were best friends and they lived in the UK. They both lost their parents in their childhood, so they were orphans and were looked after by volunteer parents. They stayed, ate, studied and played together since childhood and they were like family to each other. The two boys did not have materialistic things but they had each other and they had their fertile imagination.

Interestingly, they were both born with magical powers to become invisible. Also, they had a mysterious power to be teleported to any place they imagined. They both kept their magical powers secret from the outer world.

They went to the same school in the city of London. In one of their English lessons with Mrs. Rose, they learnt about different countries. The most inspiring country that they learnt about was UAE. They read different books about Dubai (UAE) and other countries in school in their 'Learn About the World' theme week.

They wondered how people could ski in a city which is literally a desert and they read about the tallest skyscraper, Burj Khalifa in the world is built in Dubai.

From that day, during lunch time at school, Jack and Ali decided to go on an expedition to the magical city of Dubai and other parts of the UAE. They discussed how much fun Dubai will be. They didn't have the money or permission to travel to UAE but they could use their magical powers to make their dream adventure come true.

Therefore, they made a secret plan to leave for Dubai in their spring holidays so that the teachers wouldn't notice much that they were missing and planned to tell their volunteer parents that they will be going to

Scotland to meet their relatives. They packed their bags and used their magical powers to become invisible and later they imagined their dream destination hard to use their magical powers to get teleported to Dubai but surprisingly it didn't work. They tried hard and hard and again and again, yet, to their amazement, their powers weren't working. They were about to give up on the idea of going to Dubai, when Ali came up with an exciting idea. He told Jack that they could still become invisible so why not? They boarded an Emirates flight to Dubai through Heathrow airport. Initially, Jack was reluctant as the whole plan was too adventurous for him but he agreed because he didn't want to spoil the fun they planned together. Also, he believed in his best friend's plan as Ali helped and supported him in all good and bad times all his life. Jack was horrified for this adventure, but he kept a little strong face for his friend, Ali.

The next moment, they became invisible and off they left for the airport. They sneaked through the airport and to the airplane that was supposed to fly to Dubai.

While the plane was standing, they climbed over to the wings of the plane. So, they took ropes and leashed them onto the plane. Jack feared heights, so as the plane was taking off, he was panic-stricken. On the other hand, Ali felt gallant and made Jack comfortable by distracting him. He cracked jokes and was successful in keeping Jack busy with his silliest talks. The plane finally took off.

It was a long flight and up there, cold winds were blowing. Jack and Ali were feeling cold but luckily, they were wearing warm clothes to keep them cozy. Up in the sky, they enjoyed picturesque and breathtaking views of the lull, beautiful blue sky. As the plane was ascending, they could see the houses more and smaller. The boats and ships that were sailing in River Thames looked like toy boats from up there. They could see a tiny London bridge, and the London Eye also looked too small.

A few minutes later, all they could see was the white, fluffy clouds and they were surrounded by them. The two friends took out some snack bars from their pockets and they started munching them. After a while, Jack and Ali dozed off.

A few hours later, when they woke up, they saw the huge brown sand dunes down there and a huge, dark blue tranquil ocean below them. The plane was slowly descending, and they could see tall buildings and then Ali pointed towards the Burj Khalifa.

Suddenly, they saw a few parachutes and surprisingly a few people skydiving just up from the tallest building in the world.

They were very excited to see the Dubai frame and Burj Al Arab. Jack finally looked happy as if he overcame his fears. "How brave are they to jump off the plane to skydive?" yelled curious Jack.

"I'm sure it will be a very thrilling and fun experience!" responded Ali.

"I would never be brave enough to even try it," added Jack.

"If you wouldn't try something then how would you know if you could do it," continued Ali, "look, how brave you are to be sitting here on a wing of a plane to go on an expedition, did you ever imagine that you would do something like this!"

"No way, I was so petrified by this whole idea! I'm so glad that I listened to you. What a lovely experience this is! I have never seen such a beautiful serene, picturesque sky before. I never felt so courageous before," explained Jack happily.

"There you go! You tried and you liked it and I'm always there for you. You are my family!" added Ali emotionally.

They were about to land at their dream destination. Jack and Ali started screaming out of excitement. As the plane was descending, Jack once again got anxious and yet again Ali grabbed his hands tightly and started talking about the bucket list that they made before setting off for this expedition, to make Jack excited about the fun stuff coming up ahead.

Finally, the plane landed, and they sneaked out of the airport. They had their bucket list ready for things to do in the UAE.

They went to different places, like Ski Dubai, Butterfly Garden, Motion Gate, Legoland, Ferrari World, Dubai Kart Auto-drome and to their favorite Sushi restaurants, and at the top of the Burj Khalifa. They had an amazing time together! Lots of giggles, shared food, thrilling rides and most importantly wonderful memories that they added to their already great friendship.

Eventually, they were exhausted and euphoric at the same time. Sadly, It was time to return back home. So, they thought about returning and luckily this time around they were teleported back to London that very instant. Both boys were quite surprised that their magical powers worked this time and not before.

Jack said, "Maybe we were meant to experience the flight to overcome our fear."

Ali laughed and replied, "Wouldn't you agree that going on that plane the way we did was the best part of our expedition?"

"Spot on!" laughed Jack.

The next moment, Ali and Jack fell off to sleep as they were extremely tired from their long adventurous journey!

Stories

by

- Year Four -

Arianna Dhillon

Olamide Lawore

Sophie and her Best Friend GiGi, the Giraffe

by Arianna Dhillon

They had always been together, for as long as he could remember. They had been the best of friends. She had taught him everything he knew, relentlessly preparing him for life in the outside world. This is the moment they had been waiting for ....

Let me take you back to how they first met....

One day a girl called Sophie was skipping across a forest singing her favourite tiktok dance song, she learnt with her sister. "Green Green Grass, Blue Blue Sky," and all of a sudden, she saw the brightest turquoise light, gleaming from the sky. She blocked her eyes with her forearm, because the light nearly blinded her, then she heard the loudest THUD right in front her feet. She was trembling from head to toe, as she was terrified of what had fallen right next to her feet. She slowly lifted her forearm, and was shocked to see a baby giraffe with googly eyes beyond her feet.

Sophie was very confused about where it came from and how that giraffe appeared from a bright light and a loud thud. There was a lot of suspicious activity going on.

Sophie found the giraffe adorable and cute, like a little puppy. So, she knelt down and started stroking its fluffy light - tan skin, while admiring his big brown googly eyes. ☺ She was not scared any more, quite the opposite. She wanted to keep the giraffe forever.

She had a gazillion thoughts in her head. Should I take the giraffe home? 'But my parents won't let me keep it.' Her mum would be furious! But if she left the giraffe, who was going to take care of him and feed him? Where would he sleep? Will he be ok by himself? Does he know how to take care of himself? He is just a baby; I don't want to leave him. He's very cute and I really want to take care of it. I think I could sneak him in the house, but I think it's only a matter of time until my parents find out. They know everything about me. My mummy says she has eyes at the back of her head, but I don't really believe her, because I never even see them! So, if I can't see them, how am I supposed to believe her?'

'Well, I have decided, I'm going to take the giraffe to my house.' Sophie thought. 'I feel responsible for him because I found him, and I was the only one that has seen him in this area of the world. As giraffes normally live in the Savannah, I don't live there, I live in Australia.'

So, Sophie took him home and hid him at first, but she couldn't keep a secret for long and she told mum and dad and she showed them the newest member of our family. Her parents were shocked, surprised, confused, literally all, the things you can think off. She called her cute little giraffe, Gigi.

Then a few years later, he was all grown up and he was really tall but no one knew Gigi lived with the family, except for Sophie's mum and dad. They did everything together, playing, eating, sleeping, but not going to school! No one else could ever know about Gigi because he was an alien giraffe, that popped out of nowhere.

One day Sophie was walking around the town and she saw a sign saying, 'Show your unique pets for a chance to win a gold sparkling trophy!'

Sophie started squealing with excitement and ran back home and told her parents. She then she sat with GiGi thinking about what unique skills GiGi had, that might help them win. She then started singing and dancing to her favourite tiktok song "Green Green Grass, Blue Blue Sky," to help her think and get some creative ideas.

GiGi all of a sudden, copied the exact same moves that Sophie did, and sang the song. Sophie couldn't believe her eyes, so she started training GiGi by helping him learn how to dance to the whole song by heart and all the other tiktok songs you can imagine.

Sophie and GiGi had been practising all day and night because they wanted to win the gold, sparkling, gleaming, precious trophy.

A few days later, it was the day of the show, Sophie was so excited and she believed she and Gigi could win. She got GiGi all dressed up and ready for the show. This was the day they had been waiting for... they had worked day and night for this. Sophie had done everything to make sure Gigi was ready for life outside the world and ready to perform in front of everyone.

It was their turn to perform. Sophie and Gigi were both excited and scared! They were on stage in their beautiful, sparkly, matching girl and boy outfits. The music began, Sophie and Gigi started dancing and singing. The crowd started clapping and dancing along. No matter what, nothing would stop them, they thought they would win the prize after the show, but then they actually won the great big grand, gold trophy. They couldn't believe it! The crowd gave a big round of applause and started throwing bouquets of flowers onto the stage.

After that, she had the happiest life with her

parents, and Gigi. A few years later, GiGi told Sophie he wanted to go home to see his parents. Sophie was sad but excited, as she might be able to go to space because GiGi was from space! So, they both make a plan to go to space to find his mum and dad.

Oh, I forgot to tell you... but when Sophie saw the bright turquoise light, when she first saw GiGi, she also saw a UFO just above it, so that is why she wanted to travel to space to find his parents.

Sophie and GiGi had a bond and a relationship that could never separate them. So, she really wanted to help him, as she knew it would make him really happy, and they would always be friends no matter where they lived.

Sophie and GiGi worked on their plan, and after dawn, it was ready! So first, she would have to make an astronaut suit and a space rocket to fly into space with her and GiGi.

Then she would travel across all the galaxies in the universe to find his parents. Well in her opinion, she thinks that she probably can't travel across the universe is because it will take 1 million years, unless she finds a wormhole!

The backup plan was, instead of building her own rocket, she would go to the closest space station, sneak in and collect an astronaut suit and a space rocket. When she's in the rocket she will fly off to outer space with GiGi to find his parents.

The next week, she snuck in the space station and her plan was successful. She got Gigi back to his parents, but she was sad because she made loads of memories with him, well at least he got to be with his parents again. They were the best of friends and they would always stay in touch using zoom and messages and stuff.

After that, she went home and had a really nice dinner and had fun with her parents. She was so happy she made friends with a giraffe and that she was the "only one" in the world who had who became best friends with a giraffe, and they both lived happily ever after.

Nico, the Timid Giraffe

by Olamide Lawore

They had always been together, for as long as he could remember. They had been the best of friends. She had taught him everything he knew, relentlessly preparing him for life in the outside world! This was the moment they had both been waiting for where they could be free to run wild............

Little did they know that moment was to come sooner than they thought.

It all started that morning when Esme and her brother Nico went on a walk. Esme had chestnut colour skin and velvety, coiled hair.

Nico was a tall, timid giraffe. They were orphans and they lived in the magical town of Enobis, however, Nico had a difficult past.

Weeks ago, a fairy named Firela cursed Nico and turned him into a giraffe saying that if he wanted to be healed, he would have to find the magical Edeni fruit which was located in the disenchanted forest.

As soon as the sun fairies came up the next day, Esme and Nico decided to go on an adventure. They knew where they were going and they knew they had to go quickly...

Once they were done packing, Esme and Nico set out. "Hello, world!!" They both yelled.

Their first destination was a beautiful patch of land and flowers. Nico enjoyed picking out the leaves from the top of the trees, and Esme enjoyed munching on the various types of berries and fruits, which reminded her of her wooden cottage back at home.

Next, they went to the hot springs, and then to a relaxing lazy river. Since Nico couldn't fit he decided to munch on the leftover leaves by the riverside while Esme swam. After a relaxing first day of their adventure, they knew it was time to start their mission, so they made their way to the disenchanted forest.

Hours later, tired and exhausted, Esme and Nico found the guardian of the Edeni fruit.

"We seek the Edeni fruit!" Esme yelled feeling flustered.

"And whom may I ask are you? the Guardian asked.

"We are Esme and Nico Walitine of Enobis, we come bearing gifts!" Esme said while giving the guardian a fruit.

"This is the rare albino apple! I accept your offer, here is the magical fruit!" the Guardian boomed. Nico decided to eat the fruit later when it blossomed.

A couple of hours later, they finally found a quiet place to settle down. They put up their tents and went to sleep. Once they woke up, Nico sighed with regret, "Esme, I only have a couple of days left as a Giraffe, so let's start heading back home."

"But what if we find a new home? Let's explore the entire world if we want!" Esme yelled.

"Perfect!" Nico beamed while lifting his head, and so they set out.

Nico and Esme considered many places. First a tropical, gigantic jungle, but that was too humid. There was also an evergreen forest, but there were far too many animals to share that place with.

Days went by and finally, they found a new home which was a lush and lively area surrounded by rolling green hills and a plethora of flowers from white daisies to pink tulips. They nodded to each other and decided this was the place. They found a lovely cottage that they made their home.

In the morning, they realised it was Nico's last day as a giraffe, so Nala spent the entire day picking the tallest leaves in the trees and laughing with Esme. At the end of the day, before they went to sleep, Nico pulled out the fruit, ate it and said goodbye to his giraffe-self but nothing happened. After waiting patiently for a long time, they started to wonder if the magic of the Edeni could really save Nico, but decided to stay hopeful and go to sleep. They smiled at each other, saying, "see you soon!"

And in the morning, he turned into a boy a blue smoke appeared and hid him when he came out he had puffy black hair chocolate skin and a glistening smile. His eyes were blue and he had rosy cheeks.

"Esme!" Nico yelled while hugging his sister.

"Nico, you're finally yourself again!" Esme sobbed.

"I know and I missed being a boy!" Nico grinned while wiping his sister's tears, and they ran into the sunset where they could be free to run wild......

Stories

by

- Year Five -

Subhana Bint Shahid

Mazen Hameed

Sara Bal

Natalia Cordeiro Dsouza

Aiza Nabil Salim

Alaia Rasheed

Mihika Gautam

Kings' School Al Barsha

A Journey of a Lifetime

by Subhana Bint Shahid

They had always been together for as long as he could remember. She had taught him everything he knew, relentlessly preparing him for the life of the outside world! This was the moment they had been waiting for...

Honey and Lacey were leaving their home on a mission of a lifetime. Honey was a tall spotty giraffe who had a strong heart. He had been living with his owner Lacey for as long as he could remember.

Lacey was a strong girl with a golden waterfall of hair that cascaded down her back. She was going to take Honey to the Savannah where his natural habitat was. The Savannah was located on the east.

They had to pack a lot of food and water, since it was a long journey that lasted a couple of long hours. They had to cross a river into the valley and reach the other side, where the savannah was. It was hot and windy, and the dryness made honey eat and eat more than he should have had while crossing the river. It was hard work, but they managed to cut down a tree and used it as a bridge to cross the river.

Just as they reached the valley, Lacey realised something. "OH NO! we ran out of food and water!" She then looked at Honey noticing his cheeks were full. "Oh Honey," sighed Lacey.

They walked on silently as they crossed the chilly, damp mists of the valley. Halfway through, Lacey spotted something looming in the shadows behind a rock.

"Wait here," Lacey said to Honey, and she hurried over to it. Lifting the surprisingly cold rock that weighed down her fingers, she saw a squirrel, it looked at Lucy, took an astonished squeak and leaped behind another rock. Lacey lifted that rock and to her confusion she saw two squirrels. They squeaked noisily and the two left behind another rock.

Lacey lifted that rock and saw three squirrels. "What's wrong?" she asked.

The squirrels looked at each other and one of them chittered and explained that there was no food or water for them. Thinking quickly, she ran over to Honey who was now snoozing, grabbed a water bag, went to the clean side of the valley and she found a crystal-clear pond of water. Scooping it up, she put it in the water bag and brought it to the squirrels and she said, "We'll find some food later, can you show us the way to the Savannah?"

The squirrels nodded and scampered off leading the way - after stopping for food - and then they continued through the valley to a place they had never been before.

Wearily, Lacey and the animals padded through the night. The sky was beginning to grow as black as a crow and all of them were starting to feel hungrier than ever. It seemed an impossibility that they would ever reach their final destination. Utter exhaustion had set in and Lacey suggested that they all should take a brief rest. When they awoke, dawn had begun to break. They quickly discovered they had reached the end of the Savannah without realizing.

Lacey was the first one to get up and she was astonished by what she saw before her very eyes. Hurriedly, she woke up the others and they too were mesmerized by what they saw. All of them huddled together to admire this beautiful scene. They could see the sun as an orange flame rising up the horizon, spreading warmth through their bodies. It was a beautiful sight.

They trotted on, walking through the plains as the sun slowly rose into the air. "Let's wander about and see this amazing place," Lacey squeaked excitedly as she was eager to explore.

So off everyone went, in their own direction, (except for the squirrels, since they knew where they were going as they lived in the Savannah). Lacey was sprinting through the grass while Honey was feasting on a huge amount of tree leaves that he found.

Suddenly, the sky began to grow as dark the clouds huddled together to become one big cloud, then there was a BOOM! And a flash of light that scared Lacey right out of her skin. She looked back and saw Honey's family running away from lightning. "OH NO!" Lacey cried.

Just after she said 'oh no', a humongous herd of animals darted (like bullets) toward Honey's family. The animals rescued them, and everyone was cheerful again. Then the sky became lighter, and everyone could see the bright sky. It wasn't just that, food became to grow and rain came filling up water ponds.

As for Lacey, she grew up to become a safari keeper. They lived happily ever after.

An Everlasting Connection

by Mazen Hameed

They had always been together, for as long as he could remember. They had always been the best of friends. She taught him everything he knew, relentlessly preparing him for life in the outside world! This was the moment they had both been waiting for...

Anxious, apprehensive Gerald, leaned his long neck over the barn door, his thoughts in complete turmoil.

Memories flashed across his mind like bolts of lightning. As far as he could remember, it was Grace and him. Grace had been his first teacher, first caregiver, first friend. They had grown up together – racing in the giraffe enclosure, teasing the gorillas, chasing the zebras, and chatting with the monkeys. It was Grace who taught him the tricks of the trade – how to look out for danger, which leaves had the tastiest food and who to trust. You see, Grace's father owned this zoo and the family worked extremely hard to keep the facilities in decent shape.

Gerald was a tiny baby when he came into Mr. Johnson's Zoo. With the family's nurturing care, he had now grown into an adolescent. Space was tight. Grace had prepared him – he knew that one day he would no longer fit in the zoo and would have to be released into the wild.

Initially, Gerald was terribly upset and a little jealous too. He thought he was being replaced by someone younger. That the Johnson family did not love him anymore. His heart broke into a million pieces at that thought. Eyes tearful, he knew that not to be true. Grace had promised she would always hold him in her heart. Forever.

Now, as the night progressed, he could not rest. Would he survive in the wild? Would he find his birth family? Would he be missed in the zoo?

The morning sun rose like it did every day, as if nothing special was about to happen. Someone was feeding the animals, the cleaners went about their business as usual, the vets were checking in on the animals. It was like any other day. Except for Gerald, it was not. He wanted to etch the sights and sounds of the zoo in his mind forever. This was his home, his safe space.

Gerald's eyes searched for Grace. 'Where was she? Why could he not see her? Ah, there she was! Sobbing in the corner. She was trying to be strong too. This must be so hard for her as well,' Gerald thought.

After breakfast, a large van noisily pulled into the driveway. It was time. Time for Gerald to go. To start his new life.

Grace walked over and gave him the longest hug. She whispered, "I will never forget you. You are my best friend. One day, we will meet again."

Soon enough, Gerald was loaded into the van and with the sudden start of the engine, they were gone! Gerald looked out of the window till Grace was but a tiny dot in the horizon.

After what felt like eternity, the van drove into the dark, damp forest. Animal sounds came from every corner - a racket compared to the quiet chatter at the zoo. Terrified, Gerald held his breath as the van lurched to a sudden stop. Now or never, thought Gerald. Taking a long pause, he stepped out of the van. His emotions contradicted. On some level, Gerald was excited to explore his new surroundings.

The first night away from the comfort of the zoo was torturous. Gerald held back tears on several occasions. The only reason he did not sob was because he wanted to prove to himself that he was brave and not a domesticated animal who had lost the ability to survive in his natural habitat.

He missed Grace. He wished for safety. With every movement, he jumped out of his skin. Not soon enough for Gerald, dawn broke. Under the bronze light of the sun, he skimmed his surroundings. Looking for anything familiar, he found Senegalia leaves and devoured them happily.

Satiated, he was going to explore and introduce himself to the other animals and make new friends.

Eventually, this forest became his home. He became less home sick as days passed. The Council of Elders taught him the laws of the forest.

After a while, his time at the zoo felt like a faraway dream – like that was a parallel universe.

Having spent fifteen years in the forest, Gerald was a veteran. He had taken many newbies under his wing, clearly remembering the terror he felt in his early days. Occasionally he would think of Grace and wonder how she was doing and what she had made of her life.

Then one day, a brown-haired woman stepped out of a van. The van brought back a slew of memories. Was there a new giraffe being brought into the forest? It did not seem like that... This felt different. The woman stirred emotions in Gerald's mind, and he felt a deep connection that he could not explain. Curiosity got the better of him and Gerald approached the van, against all the advice that was being shouted at him from his friends.

The woman must have felt something too as she ran across to him. "Gerald!!" she exclaimed. It was Grace!!! He knew it in his bones!

She had kept his promise and found him!

It was time for the old friends to reconnect and reminisce.

Some friendships, no matter the time or distance, always remain close to the heart.

The Device

by Sara Bal

Without warning, the flame disappeared, as did the two boys! When the flame reappeared, the boys could not believe where they were...

Both boys were amazed. Flying rocks, the size of a large room, were drifting in the air peacefully and wild, golden lightning bolts clashed down to the planet's surface. The sky changed colour every time the lightning clashed – ultramarine blue, then to sea-foam green and finally to amethyst teal.

Various types of majestic bubbles were emerging from the ground as if it was like the sea combined with the world's surface.

The boys were disorientated. Flying past them were sea creatures such as sea horses, octopus and jellyfish. The sea horses were smaller than the boys' hands, yet the octopus was larger than a bus and strangely had a balloon attached to each tentacle. Strangest of all were the jellyfish which changed color and each one had its own unique pattern on its head. Liam and Jacob had mixed feelings about this world. Scared and frightened, excited and astonished - will they ever reach home and if so, how?

Searching frantically for shelter, tears began to form in their hazel eyes as they almost gave up hope seeking a safe place to rest. Faces dull, both boys were tired and exhausted by this crazy dimension. Neither of them knew how long they had been here – was it ten hours or was it an eternity?

Eventually, the boys found a cave that could be used for shelter. Jacob grabbed some pointy brown materials which looked like wood and started to make a fire. As he rubbed the strange material together, sparks of purple light glistened in the darkness around him, which reminded him of his chemistry class. Meanwhile, Liam used thick, long leaves to make a shelter that he hoped would protect them from the continuing storms and rain. Both boys knew that it was going to be a rough night ahead of them, but they were not apprehensive about this as they had camped many times by themselves in jungles, rainforests and mountains all over the world.

As the three moons rose up over the horizon, they formed into one humungous, dazzling sun – signaling the start of a new day on this strange earth. Red bloodshot eyes indicated that the boys had a restless night, yet their shelters had protected them from the storms, even though their fire had been blown out during the early hours. Wearily, they soon started to head off to somewhere they did not know.

Liam and Jacob had been walking for hours searching for food and anything that looked safe to drink. In the distance, both boys were suddenly aware of heavy thunder clashes ahead of them.

"Do you think we should go and check out that storm?" asked Liam.

Jacob looked curious. "Sure," he replied, "but we should be careful."

As the boys walked closer to the storm, they heard noises coming from above them. Frozen in fear, the boys suddenly realised where the thunder was coming from. Above their heads, they saw two, tall, slim men standing on lightning bolts up high fighting for the lives. One man was covered with a dark blue cloak and the other was covered in a deep red cloak. Behind the men stood two grand castles – one made of crystal blue ice and the other was made of flaming red fire.

"I wonder if those castles belong to them," suggested Jacob.

"It looks to me that they are defending them," responded Liam, "we should stay out of their way, they look dangerous."

Icy bolts of lightning and steaming hot fire bolts continued to be thrown in the air until suddenly everything stopped. It was then when both boys, Jacob and Liam, found the two men staring down at them – unblinking, the men's eyes looked cold and frozen as they glared down at the boys.

Fear running down their faces, Liam and Jacob nodded to each other, and in a split second both boys tore apart and went their separate ways. Running for the lives, both boys didn't look back once! Liam and Jacob knew this would be their only chance of survival if they separated.

Fire was zooming past Jacob as he dodged each bolt until he ran out of breath. Behind him was the cloaked man in red who was clearly frustrated with rage as his face was glowing with fire. On the other side of the forest, Liam was stuck with the man dressed in blue, who continued to throw ice and snow down to the forest floor below him.

As both men grew tired of chasing the boys, Liam and Jacob took the opportunity to find a safe place to hide. Liam was hidden in a small wet cave and Jacob was hiding behind a strange purple tree, large enough for him to hide inside.

As the day passed by, both boys remained in their hiding places – Liam in the cave and Jacob inside the tree. The strange men did not give up their search easily, however they soon grew tired and left later that evening

Relieved, the boys began to calm down but knew that it would not be easy to find each other in this dense forest. Separately, they decided to rest for the night as they had still not eaten that day and were incredibly hungry and tired. The cave and the tree allowed Liam and Jacob to sleep peacefully compared to their first night.

The next morning, both boys woke up, thinking that this was all a crazy dream until they opened their eyes and found themselves waking up in the familiar cave and tree. As the younger brother, Jacob, felt terrified that he was all alone in this never-ending dimension. He began to cry.

On the other side of the forest, in his small, damp cave, Liam thought about his younger brother. He felt sad that he had left his brother all alone. As he reached into his pocket to get a tissue, Liam's hand touched something. Then he remembered! In the palm of his hand, he withdrew the device that he had created in his physics class. Had it really worked? The circular device that spiraled up to a central button hummed quietly in Liam's hand. He knew what he had to do. With newfound encouragement, Liam set off to find his younger brother.

Far off in the distance, Jacob wondered if his brother was safe. He stood up, wiped away his tears and climbed out of the tree. Jacob started to wander off in search of his older brother. Both boys retraced their steps after they had split up the previous day. They had been walking for most of the morning and eventually found themselves at the same place as where their adventure had begun. They could not believe their eyes when they found each other later that day. At first, they stood still, just staring, but after a few minutes they hugged each other.

Liam apologised to Jacob that it had all been his fault and it was because he had the physics device in his pocket that they had ended up here. He was also sorry for leaving Jacob alone and promised it would never happen again. Liam explained to Jacob what they needed to do. Taking Jacob's hand, they held the device and closed their eyes.

As both boys opened their eyes, they found themselves back home with their family. Liam took out the physics device and placed it on the floor. He crushed it with his foot to make sure that this mistake would never happen again.

Treasured Friends

by Natalia Cordeiro Dsouza

"Look! Look down there!" His voice could just about be heard above the sound of the aeroplane's engine and the shrieking wind in their ears.

"Can you see it?" Liam's voice screeched. He hugged the binoculars to his chest like they were a baby. He was too scared to drop them.

Luna screamed back, "WOW, yes! Yes! It's awesomely colossal and dense, what an eye-catching mosaic of trees and vegetation!"

Then, she advanced to running her waiting fingertips through the clouds. It felt like a dream. She was getting closer to the edge of the plane wing, until...

Whilst bouncing off the comforting clouds against you is nice, it isn't the best feeling to be falling through the air at a very high speed and screaming at the top of your lungs.

As Luna was falling through the sky, Liam watched his twin sister, his best friend, plummet out of sight after her parachute had blown up.

Liam had two options,

1. To call the plane down

2. To jump

He had no time to ponder. He quickly selected Option 2 and silently screaming in his head, jumped. The wind was an icy sword to his cheek as he almost froze into an ice block. The bright blue parachute puffed up as Liam decided it was a suitable time to shout and so he did!

Luna had landed in a tiny clearing and was all alone for ten whole minutes. She felt tired and dizzy with confusion. She could barely catch her breath after the long fall. Suddenly, she heard a loud shout as her brother tumbled on top of her.

After the twins stood up, Luna screamed with thrilling excitement in Liam's ears, "WE ARE IN THE AMMMAAAAZZZZOONN, YIPEEEEEEE!" It was a shout that shook the foundations of the forest, one that pierced above the trees. It was indeed their dream come true.

They looked around them and were captivated by the immense beauty, the incredibly rich flora and fauna and the enchanting sounds that surrounded them.

But, in a few seconds, the holler of happiness turned into a shriek of dismay.

"AAAAAAAAHHHHHHHHHHHHH!" yelled Liam, as it started to rain.

But the way it pattered down was mesmerizing, like a million animal paws and claws padding the ground. They swiftly ran for shelter under a tiny, kind tree.

Liam was starting to panic. He looked around to suddenly see a spider. He backed away, cowering. It had humungous legs and tangy fangs. Unexpectedly, Liam hit something.

He turned around and found a sign that read 'Junior Ranger Lodges.' Liam and Luna heaved a sigh of relief and ran in the direction of the lodges and checked into the biggest accommodation and started to explore. It had the most spectacular views from the balcony-like deck which had a rippling stream flowing below it. It was a really comfy lodge.

Eventually, it stopped raining. Now, the trees poured their water into the stream and some also splashed onto the deck. The dapples of sunshine shone through the towering, evergreen trees and the birds chirped. The trees shook in the wind.

Liam relaxed in the living area and started to read an interesting book about the Amazon, the largest rainforest on earth.

'The Amazon is home to an amazing array of fascinating plants, insects, birds, fish, mammals and deadly creatures. It is indeed a kaleidoscope of colourful sights and sounds. The rain is also a beautiful element of the rainforest. It nurses the thirsty plants and animals. The trees cleanse our atmosphere.'

While Liam was reading, he noticed Luna staring at something. Abandoning his book, he went to check. Staring out of the window, (after slumping on Luna's bed), he saw a tree stump and on the circular cylinder, was a sloth! Around the stump, there were animals and they were...TALKING to each other!

Luna and Liam could understand every word!

"Hello Otter Otto!" squawked a toucan happily, along with an orangutan, a lemur and a red-tailed squirrel. Then, Sadie the sloth 'boss' said, "It's time to pick some fruit and catch some fish. But, before we start our work for the day, there is something I want to mention. There is some unpleasant news going around in the forest. An immensely large machine has been spotted and it is cutting down our trees. We really need to do something about it." All the animals seemed to agree and then they scampered off to work.

Liam and Luna kept an eye on their favourite animal, 'Otto' the otter. Suddenly, they spotted the gigantic machine in the distance. It was crunching and clenching the trees. Gaping in horror, they watched it slowly destroying the forest cover. Then it cut down some more trees and one partly fell on Otto's legs. The pain was so bad he yelped out loud and unexpectedly passed out. The animals ran towards Otto and tried to help him. The twins hurriedly got to the site too.

"Help us!" chattered Otis the orangutan! Without wasting any time, Luna and Liam rushed with Otto and splashed him with water from the stream. Otto awoke. They tried to examine his legs and to make Otto feel comfortable.

The animal friends quickly explained to Otto how the twins had helped to revive him with their quick thinking. Otto thanked the 'Terrific Two' gratefully. He sadly narrated everything about the terrifying, petrifying machine.

Lori the Lemur and Riley the red-tailed squirrel spoke up, "How are we supposed to stop this? This dreadful machine is harming our home, our friend, our life - the forest!

How are we going to survive?"

Then Toco the toucan added, "My earlier home was destroyed, so I moved here, to this part of the forest. Now I feel miserable to see the same thing happening here too. If this continues, are we going to lose our home and our dearest, oldest, most treasured friend the rainforest?"

This made Luna and Liam ponder at that question. After this first-hand experience of the massive damage being caused and the most fascinating rainforest being destroyed inch by inch, with all the essential and wonderful elements it contains, the duo were determined to get back home and create an awareness to make a positive change.

Zoe and Her Old Friend

by Aiza Nabil Salim

They had always been together, for as long as he could remember. They had always been the best of friends. She had taught him everything she knew, relentlessly preparing him for life in the outside world! This was the moment they had both been waiting for... it was time to set her free.

It all started when Zoe's dad had told her that he had some work to do in Africa for six months so she would have to come with her.

At first, Zoe wasn't sure she would have to leave school and adapt to a different home. Then her dad told her that the trip was going to be fun and they will have an animal safari every once in a while. He also told her that he promised her teacher that he would bring school work for Zoe to catch up.

Zoe finally decided to go on the trip to Africa. Their flight was on the following Tuesday (two more days until the flight).

Zoe's mom had divorced, and she never saw her after that. Even though the flight was in two days, it felt like an eternity. As the days passed, Zoe began packing in her small yellow suitcase. She packed:

- Twelve pairs of socks
- Fifteen t-shirts
- Three pairs of shoes
- Ten trousers
- Two shorts
- Two hats
- Sunscreen
- A swimsuit
- Stationery
- A camera
- A series of books
- Five packs of her favorite biscuits
- Six jars of maple syrup
- Three bottles of mango juice

The day of the flight arrived, her dad woke her up and told her to change and come downstairs. She quickly changed, grabbed her suitcase and dragged it down the stairs, almost tripping over it.

"Have some breakfast because we're leaving in ten minutes," grunted her dad. Zoe walked towards the fridge and grabbed some milk and poured it into her cereal bowl. After she was finished, she got into the car and her dad drove off. The car shuddered along the bone shaking trail. Clouds of dust sprayed the windscreen as the road began to narrow.

In the distance, Zoe could see the outline of the airport and before you knew it, they were at the airport finding a parking space, which wasn't that easy because unfortunately, most flights flew in the middle of the night. Eventually they found a spot and got their suitcases out. They climbed up the escalator and found the waiting area for their flight.

Suddenly, they heard a ding which meant it was time to board the plane. The pair found their seats and Zoe sat in the window seat. Zoe felt tired so she went to sleep as her dad ate his breakfast. Once Zoe had woken up, she looked outside the window and down there, she saw colossal trees joined together like a crowd of vivid green umbrellas and the emerald surface of the sea glittering with a million diamonds of sunlight.

The flight was seven hours long but finally they reached Africa, got out of the plane and booked a taxi to the large hut that they were staying in. Once they reached the wooden house, Zoe found a room and thrust her suitcase onto her bed. It was 10:00 A.M and Zoe was already feeling bored. So, she decided to explore the savannah a little bit.

She told her dad she was going exploring and her dad said, "You can't go unless you come back in one hour."

Zoe nodded, swung the door open and slammed it shut. She walked past some shrubs, stepped over twisted branches and walked around the thorn bushes until she saw a hill towering over her. Suddenly, she heard a loud MMMMMMMMRRRRRR.

She ran up the hill but didn't see anything except for trees, bushes an sand but in out of the corner of her eye she saw a creature running towards the other side. She decided it would be hopeless looking for it because first of all, she most likely wouldn't find it. Second of all, she would probably get lost and third of all, she is not a fast runner and even if she did try to chase it, the creature could probably harm her or run away from her. So she decided to go back home and search the next day.

She walked towards the wooden house and asked her dad if any animals lived in the savannah. He said that there weren't any animals around here because this place was deserted. Zoe said OK even though she didn't quite believe her dad. She walked towards her room and took a jar of maple syrup from under her bed. Then she sprinted towards the kitchen, opened a cupboard and took out a spoon.

She went back into her room and started to eat maple syrup (her favourite food) with a spoon. After a few moments, her dad called her for dinner which was salad. Zoe told her dad that she would finish her salad in her room.

"Just make sure that you don't put maple syrup on your salad like you always do!" yelled Zoe's dad.

"Ok fine," she lied.

The first thing she did when she got into her room was to pour maple syrup onto her salad. She found it delicious and finished it in a blink. She loved maple syrup so much she would have cereal with maple syrup instead of milk!

The next day, once she finished eating breakfast, she was going to ask her dad if she could go exploring but he was not there. She looked in her room, in his room and in the office but he was nowhere to be seen. She never ever thought that her dad would leave her alone in a wooden house that she had only been in for about two days.

She looked in the storage room and realised she was right when she thought that her dad would never abandon her in a wooden house. He was in the storage room.

"Can I go exploring again and can I bring maple syrup with me in case I get hungry," pleaded Zoe.

"Yes of course! you can," said her dad.

"Thank you!" Zoe exclaimed.

Hurriedly, she went outside and walked towards the hill. She climbed up the steep hill and waited for the MMMMMMMMRRR. She waited and waited until she realised that the creature would never come. But just as she was heading to leave, she heard it, MMMMMMMRRRR. She looked back and saw a big, tall giraffe but there was something green tied to its leg.

Zoe cautiously walked down the hill making sure she didn't frighten it. Gallantly, she walked as slow as a snail toward the giraffe. Then suddenly, Zoe was just an inch away from the giraffe. She began to try and untie the knot, but it was extremely tight. She looked at the giraffe who looked extremely hungry and then the giraffe stared at the maple syrup.

Helplessly, Zoe opened the jar using the opener and fed it to the giraffe which suddenly gave her an idea, she used the cap opener to cut the knot. It worked! But all of a sudden the giraffe shouted MMMMMRRRRR. She tried to calm the giraffe by giving it more maple syrup, which worked out well.

Zoe had just realized that this giraffe had to be named. She thought and thought and finally came up with Gilly the giraffe! Zoe wondered how this giraffe had gotten here, there was no food here and the place was deserted. She knew very well that this giraffe needed to be taken to a wildlife conservatory to be away from the dangers of any poachers. After that, she began to prepare the giraffe for the wildlife conservatory.

As the days passed, their friendship grew stronger until the last week that Zoe would be staying in Africa. Zoe used to spend all her time with Gilly as if she owned it for ages. Gilly used to wake up Zoe by tapping its head into Zoe's room window as early as the sunrise and stayed with her playing and grazing until the sunset.

Meanwhile, Zoe found a suitable wildlife conservatory for Gilly and she emailed the conservatory to come here to rescue the giraffe. Zoe didn't want to leave the giraffe in the conservatory but she needed to do the best for Gilly.

Finally, the day came. The truck had arrived to collect the giraffe. It took a century to explain what was going on to her dad. Before Gilly could go, Zoe gave her the biggest hug ever and the rest of her maple syrup. "Goodbye Gilly," Zoe cried.

She waved at Gilly until she could not see her anymore.

Now it was time for Zoe to go back home. On the plane, she vowed to herself that she would never ever forget Gilly under any circumstances as she was the best friend she could ever have.

The Land of Onieros

by Alaia Rasheed

As they stood there silently in the darkness, neither of them could have imagined what would happen next. They found the lantern by chance as they were scouring the streets looking for food.

Lying on the cobbled street, waiting to be found, the lantern burnt through the dim light of evening. The boys held it in their hands, watching the orange flame flicker in the breeze.

Without warning the flame disappeared as did the two boys!

When the flame reappeared, the boys could not believe where they were ...

It was eerily quiet, not a single soul was to be seen, the night sky so dark and vast looking bigger that the entire universe. The stars in the sky were specks of gold illuminating the ebony forest, which the boys had found themselves in. The trees of the forest were taller than the highest mountains and the floor beneath smelled of fresh earth whilst cold mist surrounded them.

Suddenly, the boys heard a sound coming from the distance. The twosome were unsure what that sound was and where it was coming from. Then the boys noticed that the shuffling sounds were now approaching them rapidly. The two brothers decided to be bold so they walked forward to where they thought the sound was coming from and then they saw it; it was a man with a cloak as long as the river Thames and white beard the colour of snow. He wore all black and was armed with a magical staff.

Next to the man there were two twin girls, one on each side. The man then spoke. "My name is Embero, the Wizard and guardian of this forest," he softly whispered, "who may you be?"

"Hello Sir Embero, my name is Calem and this is my twin brother Caleb," replied one of the brothers, "also, who are the two girls standing with you and most importantly where are we?"

"Ah yes, these are my two twin daughters Annasille and Callesta," he said. "Right now you are in the forest of Oneiros, where all your dreams come true. The two of you have been summoned to help my daughters on an important mission that's why I came, I sensed you were here."

While saying this the Wizard pulled a mysterious smile. "Your task is going to be a dangerous one full of magic so you must be smart on your actions," stated Embero. "You have to defeat the witch Esmerelda, this witch is... my sister!"

The boys were shocked and the twin girls stared at their feet. The wizard explained that his younger sister was actually a good witch but was under a curse that made her very evil and made her do awful things. The children's job was to go and take the curse off her. The Wizard told them this was only possible if they won a duel against Esmerelda, which would take a lot of power.

"Excuse me Embero, but I have a question. If we don't have any powers how will we defeat your sister?" asked Caleb. But instead of the wizard speaking, young Annasille did.

She replied, "Well actually my sister Callesta and I, have powers and we're even trained by aunt Esme so we know all her spells."

Then Callesta added, "I shall now call the

dragons one is a fire element and one water, there's Flame and Aqua. Are you ready to join us now?"

Little did Calem and Caleb know at that point they were just being introduced to their future best friends with whom they would embark on legendary adventures. Caleb and Calem took one look at each other and then nodded. Suddenly Callesta and Annasille whistled as loud as they could and then as fast as lightning, Aqua and Flame appeared. They got on the dragons after a short explanation on how to ride them and soon they were off.

"Bye father!" shouted the sisters.

"See you after we win Embero!" cried the brothers.

As the team were flying over Onieros, they noticed that dawn was approaching and while watching the sunrise they saw magical sights. There were mountains standing tall and bold towering over everything. The never-ending, turquoise lake shone gleefully in the light of dawn and they saw many unique creatures never seen before. Far ahead of them the boys caught something in the corner of their eyes, it was an onyx coloured castle with turrets touching the clouds and very few windows of which didn't take any reflection of light on them.

"Annasille, Callesta is that where your aunt is right now?"

"Yes," responded the girls, "however that's too far for the dragons to fly and there will be no place for them to land, we shall take the Phoenix's instead - the special ones," they said this with a gleam in their eyes.

"What's the difference between a normal Phoenix and a special one if you don't mind me asking and why take the special ones not the normal ones?"

"Well, the difference is that normal species are made of fire and as you know water can take fire out this will make our Phoenix's energy and power run low which would be bad if we need them for battle that wouldn't be good but the special species are made of pure magic and nothing can harm them even Aunt Esme's spell won't hurt them," elucidated Callesta.

Soon, the dragons landed and the foursome went to get their phoenixes. Luckily, the girls already were friends with the Phoenixes so there was no problem with getting on them and flying to Esmerelda's castle.

While on the phoenixes, they flew over the sapphire blue ocean and the smell of sea salt reached their nostrils. Thirty minutes later, they had reached Esmerelda's castle. By now the two brothers and two sisters started to enjoy each other's company and had one thing in common, they were not scared to take up the unknown. The group approached the castle going closer and closer but then there was a problem. The castle was under a protection spell so no one could get in. The friends took a long time to brainstorm ideas about getting in when Annasille thought of something brilliant, the sisters could merge some of their powers to take the protection spell off and the boys could try focusing on all the good times they had to strengthen the powers of the girls, after all, it is the land of dreams. With all they could do in magic, they used it and soon were able to take down the protection forcefield! Thus was the power of their friendship.

As stealthy as ninjas, the best friends walked into the castle. They weren't scared because they knew the power of their friendship would overtake Esmerelda's curse. The children went through the winding tunnels of the castle but soon another problem came along. They were lost! But then a light bulb went off in Calem's head, he asked the girls if they knew a tracking spell and the girls said yes. So Annasille and Callesta cast the tracking spell and then a path of shimmering sparkles appeared in front of the foursome. This path led them to the library. It was huge with books sitting on every shelf.

From the corner of their eyes, they saw someone approaching them. It was Esmerelda! She wore a long ebony velvet dress and had an onyx gem staff.

"Hello Annasille and Callesta," she whispered in raspy voice. "Why are you here? I never asked to you to come!"

"Well Aunt Esme, we have come to break your curse!" shouted Annasille,

"Well to do that you must duel me...NOW!" replied Esmerelda while sending a blast of magic at the kids.

The kids were thrown against the wall with the force of the magic.

The duel had begun!

The children sent their powers back at Esme and the witch fell backwards. It was a long battle but then the children cast a spell relying on their friendship as that spell was powered by it and once the spell was cast, ferocious sparks appeared.

Esmerelda was freed from the curse! Her ebony black dress became the colour of snowflakes and her onyx magical staff turned into a diamond one. Soon after, Esmerelda realised what had happened and she apologized for all the wrong that she had done.

The children returned on the phoenixes with Esmerelda to Embero and he looked extremely happy. He thanked the boys and they bid farewell. Calem and Caleb told Annasille and

Callesta that they would never forget this adventure or their friendship. The girls told them they would definitely meet again.

In the blink of an eye, the boys were suddenly back home on the same dim street where their journey had begun. Standing with the lantern, the boys remembered all the good memories they had made in Onieros, hoping they would visit there again someday.

A Hoof and a Hand

by Mihika Gautam

 Izzy was simply a normal girl, but her life was far from normal... it was very interesting and exciting. She lived with her parents, in a cottage at the edge of a beautiful, dazzling forest.

Amazingly, Izzy's parents owned the cottage and a quarter of the huge forest around it. Her hard-working dad earned money by selling wood and a rare type of coal, while her dedicated mom would sell beautiful dresses that she made.

Since Izzy's cottage was away from the hustle of the main town, she did not have any friends around to play with. She longed for friendship and companionship. She always dreamt of running up and down the meadows with a friend. Her dad sensed her loneliness and often asked her to accompany him to the forest, where she read books and finished her homework while he worked.

One such summer day, both Izzy and her dad heard a faint noise of a baby animal deep in the forest where a ferocious lion was known to reside.

Undoubtedly, they were scared but still, they fought their fear and went deep into the forest to help the animal in need.

Soon, they reached the site from where the worrying noise was coming. "Daddy, look there!" said Izzy astonished. There, right in front of them, was a cute little giraffe but the poor thing was stuck in a thorn bush.

"Looks like it has lost its way in the woods..." sighed Izzy's dad glumly.

"Well then, let's help it!" pleaded Izzy.

Without warning, Izzy's voice echoed through the massive forest. Her voice was not too loud, but enough of a disruption to wake the man-eating lion up! It roared mightily. Izzy and her dad jumped in fear, but still managed to free the baby. They ran home with the poor creature, as fast as they could.

As they reached home, Izzy's dad explained the strange story to the family while Izzy gave the sweet baby some water and food.

The family decided to let Izzy foster the giraffe. Izzy named her Giselle and thus began her training to survive in the ferocious forest.

First, Izzy made an enclosure around a tree, for Giselle. Once she was done, she added greenery, a water tray, and finally, a food tray. Then she put Giselle in the spacious enclosure. Giselle took some time to warm up to the new place.

The next step for Izzy was to befriend Giselle. For that, Izzy had to be physically closer to Giselle. Nervous, Izzy stepped into the enclosure. Beads of sweat dropped from her face. She had no idea if Giselle would attack or be calm and let Izzy come close to her. But to her surprise, Giselle was very calm around Izzy. She even came close and rubbed her nose on Izzy's cheeks. Izzy knew she had found her new best friend. Carefully and slowly, Izzy helped Giselle get up and they started walking around the enclosure.

"Okay Giselle," Izzy started, "the next step is jogging, which is basically sped up walking! So, it's not that hard. Let's start with small, baby steps... then we'll start speeding up. Does that sound good?"

Before Izzy knew it, Giselle started running like never before. "Good job Giselle!" Izzy encouraged, "Go faster!" Just as she said that, Giselle halted and came closer to Izzy and bent forward as if she was asking Izzy to get on to her back.

Picking up the cue, Izzy got on to Giselle's back. Giselle's eyes widened and gleamed and there she went running at full speed, running up and down the meadows. It was like Izzy's dream was finally coming true.

As the days passed, Giselle and Izzy's friendship grew deeper and stronger.

One day while Izzy was training Giselle, her dad stopped by. "That is one heck of a fast giraffe you've got there Izzy!" shouted Izzy's dad whilst coming down towards them.

"I know dad... she is very, very fast," replied Izzy laughing.

"You know, I feel that she is almost ready for the wild... she can run fast, she can jump, she is aware of all the dangers and understands the jungle protocol very well now. She basically has all qualities she needs to survive out there... I think in a few more days, she will be completely ready for the ferocious forest!" Izzy's dad added.

Izzy, who was very shocked, said "What? Dad, surely you can't be serious! I mean, I'll miss her and she-"

"Izzy," her dad interrupted, "she belongs to the wild. You cannot keep her here forever. Think about it, okay?" he said as he began to walk back up to the cottage.

Tears came to Izzy's eyes, as she started giving a thought on her dad's words.

The next day, Izzy walked up to her dad and said, "I feel you are right, dad. Giselle is ready for the wild. We'll take her back to the forest.".

"Are you sure? There's no rush," asked her dad.

"Yes, I'm sure dad. I don't want to be selfish," Izzy said, fighting her tears.

With a heavy heart, Izzy went to Giselle's enclosure. She hugged Giselle and said, "I am going to take you back to where you rightfully belong. It's a beautiful world out there Giselle. I'm sure you'll make lots of friends in the jungle. Just remember everything I taught you, okay?" Tears shot down from her eyes as fast as meteorites, as poor Izzy cried her little heart out. Giselle looked puzzled and clueless.

A few minutes later, Izzy got up and told herself, "Be strong Izzy, for Giselle."

Izzy and Giselle started following Izzy's dad to the forest. Roughly twenty minutes later, they arrived at a giraffe-friendly spot deep in the forest.

"Time to say goodbye Izzy," said her dad.

Izzy could not believe that she would have to say bye so soon, but she was helpless.

She slowly walked towards Giselle, her eyes

moist. They had always been together, for as long as she could remember from that day, she had helped Giselle. They had always been the best of friends. She had taught her everything she knew, relentlessly preparing her for life in the outside world! This was the moment they both had hoped for.

"Go Giselle. Run free! I hope fate will make us meet again," Izzy cried and ran into her father's arms.

Giselle soon realised what was happening and slowly, she departed into the mighty forest.

That night, Izzy cried herself to sleep. She missed Giselle more than anything!

The next morning, she hesitantly woke up to get ready for school. As she walked out of the cottage, she saw Giselle's empty enclosure. She felt a huge void in her heart. She burst into tears. Just then, she felt a nudge on her shoulders.

It was Giselle! She placed her hoof on Izzy's hand- a handshake Izzy tried hard to teach her, but always failed. This was the best surprise ever.

Izzy gave her a big hug and then jumped on to her back and off they went again. Izzy's laughter echoed all around.

From then, every morning, Giselle showed up Izzy's cottage to give her a ride to school and then patiently waited to take her back home. They played and snuggled all day and then in the evenings, Giselle went back into the forest.

Their friendship was one for the books, the one of a hoof and a hand!

Stories

by

- Year Six -

Shivaay Rohit Ramsinghani

Kiaan Ali Shah

Nandini Ram Mohan

Aarav Dave

Bissan Kadi

Honey Ava Gretton

Celena Bou Habib

Kiara Jain

Kunal Sethia

A Girl and Her Giraffe

by Shivaay Ramsinghani

They had always been together, for as long as she could remember. They had always been the best of friends. She had taught him everything he knew, relentlessly preparing him for life in the outside world. This was the moment they had both been waiting for.

"Good morning Ivar, today is the day!" announced Avianna with a mixed emotions.

But of course, Ivar only lifted and lowered his head gently. Ivar and Avianna had grown into being best of friends who had formed a truly unique bond.

Ivar was one of many giraffes at the giraffes'

sanctuary inside a large sprawling estate where caretakers would tend and rehabilitate giraffes. The sanctuary was owned and operated by Avianna's family, the Everly family. The Everly's were an aristocratic family from England with their business interests in Kenya.

Avianna's grandparents had chosen to settle in Kenya and her father had carried forward that legacy further in the country where he grew up. The Giraffe Manor, as it was named, had been founded by Avianna's grandparents. It was a generous and noble initiative from Avianna's family to give back to nature by investing their time, funds, resources and personal energy into nurturing these beautiful animals. Each generation seemed to have carried this forward gracefully.

Avianna and her sister were the next in line to this heritage. The Giraffe Manor was located in the far east region of Kenya near the picturesque wild plains. Avianna lived on the estate in a large, lavish house with her hardworking parents and her younger sister Marika, who also loved Ivar almost as much as she did. Due to the nature of work, a lot of staff were deployed to work on this estate. They carried the kindness and sweet vibration of the nature-filled, divinely connected Kenya in their services towards the giraffes. Guests from far and wide would come to see these resplendent, graceful giraffes. They would also donate money towards the maintenance and working of this noble cause and it's serene, immaculate surroundings.

Ivar had arrived at the manor years before with a tragic injury to his leg. He had been in agonising pain. During the dark days of Ivars injury, Avianna had been his only comfort, relentlessly tending to him. This unexplained instant connection and deep friendship between Ivar and Avianna felt so familiar... they both felt like old friends.

Avianna was seeking deep relationships. Since the estate was so far away, the girls could not meet friends all the time. Marika was amazing but she was not good at keeping secrets or at understanding her deeply emotional sister, so Avianna turned to Ivar, the giraffe, to become her closest confidant.

Avianna was up at dawn each morning to help her family look after the injured giraffes. Every morning, Avianna would lead Ivar to the majestic, towering waterfall at the far end of the estate where they would hang out like friends. Ivar was the best listener she had ever met. But of course, he couldn't talk - that was the only downside.

Once back at the manor, she would give him some food along with some exclusive treatment and then move on to the other giraffes.

Avianna celebrated this sweet friendship and communication with an animal. Ivar's energy was uplifting,

However, the Giraffe Manor Sanctuary was not a zoo. Every time a giraffe was deemed fit to return back to their natural habitat, a great celebration would be held to set them free back to where they belonged. It was a momentous occasion and a very emotional one too.

All of the caretakers and family members would parade the designated Giraffe along with pinning it's name and picture to a board of successful rescues. Avianna had frequently witnessed many of these ceremonies due to the amount of giraffes on the sanctuary.

The day that Avianna found out that Ivar had to leave was an emotional rollercoaster for her. Her parents sat her down in their cozy study which was lined with towering book shelves, whilst a candle was lit on the coffee-table. They tried to make it as welcoming as could but Avianna knew that whatever they had called her for would not be good. She was far too attached to Ivar and letting go would be hard.

They explained to her gently that Ivar had been there far to long. He was now fit. The team at Giraffe Manor believed that keeping Ivar there any longer would hamper his natural development. Avianna knew this day was going to come but that didn't stop her from breaking down.

Marika had tried to comfort her heartbroken sister but to no avail. Marika could hear Avianna crying herself to sleep each night knowing there was nothing she could do about it. Avianna had carried out her daily life almost like an empty shell. There was no life dancing in her eyes.

It takes months to get an animal to a mental position to go back into the wild and as Ivar had been at the sanctuary for so long the process would be challenging. Avianna had talked to Ivar for hours about this but all he did was shake his head. Both the friends seemed to be in denial.

They had to revive Ivar's natural survival instincts by the decision to release him back into the wild. Otherwise, there would be no way he could survive. Him being attached to Avianna had made it more difficult. The staff at the sanctuary had devised a transition plan for Ivar. They had to let him into the wild for a few hours each morning and gradually feed him less food at the sanctuary so that he would go look for his food in the Kenyan wilderness.

Before Avianna could fully process the feeling and come to terms with it, the day of the letting go ceremony arrived. She groomed Ivars coat until it was glistening in the morning sun and braided his hair neatly.

For the last time, Avianna took him to "their" waterfall. It was a bittersweet moment as she got her friend ready to return to his true home.

The skilled caretaker Idrissa, had gently pulled Avianna away from Ivar and led him out of his stall around the pastures of sweet smelling grass. The sun smiled brightly from up above. It was a beautiful day. They crossed the towering waterfall where they both shared secrets with each other on the rocks; although it had only been a few days since.

Avianna couldn't bear to walk Ivar herself it was to much for her already strained emotions. Ivar on the other hand also had tears rolling down his eyes. This was the sign of a deep friendship and understanding. Avianna watched from afar as Idrissa opened the leash and let Ivar out. And into the green heartland, gently trotted off Ivar...

He turned back a few times to lock eyes with Avianna telling her a silent goodbye and a heartfelt thank you for being there for him. He seemed to convey the message of "until we meet again".

Avianna's heart felt very heavy. She felt peace and happiness for her friend although she could also feel a lump in her throat and tears in her eyes. After the ceremony, Idrissa, who loved Ivar immensely as well, sat next to Avianna. They sat together for a long time in complete silence. It was dark by the time they reached back to the manor.

For the next few days, no life had returned to Avianna's eyes. Every time she crossed the caretakers office, she saw the board of rescues and couldn't bear to see the glossy picture of Ivar staring back at her. What gave her solace and the strength to move on was the understanding that she had been a sincere friend to Ivar since she had set him free to be his real self. Her parents proudly explained to her that, that was a mark of a true friend.

A few days, after Ivar left, another giraffe named Lopard, arrived at the sanctuary. She had suffered a crippling injury to her forelegs. Lopard's need for help revived Avianna's helpful and caring nature. Lopard gave the life back to Avianna just like Ivar had done although she was no match for Ivar.

Often Avianna would walk out onto the plains and softly call out for Ivar many a times. But of course, he couldn't hear his teary eyed friend's call. She learnt to replace that void with the new chapter in her life of her growing friendship with Lopard. They had always been there for each other but now Avianna had realised Ivar had gone where he and his happiness truly belonged.

She finally made peace with this cycle of life and self growth. Avianna chose to move on

by being of service to the other beautiful
giraffes that would cross her life ahead.

The Key

by Kiaan Shah

They blinked! This could not be happening. Where were they? They surveyed their surroundings. It appeared that it was early morning, about 7:00 am and they were standing on the peak of a smooth, green hill, with more of these in every direction as far as they could see. The young one, Jack, exclaimed, "Where are we Harry? I'm scared!"

"It's fine Jack, w-w-we'll be okay and we'll get back home," said the older one, Harry. More to reassure himself than Jack.

"Wait!" exclaimed Jack, pointing towards a hill southeast to them, "Over there, I see something!"

Harry followed his finger and saw some human-like figures moving in the distance in some sort of valley. "Let's go check it out," said Jack, running toward the figures while pulling Harry.

After running for what seemed like hours, they reached the valley. Jack and Harry hid behind a hill and watched the figures. It turned out they were dwarfs and not actual humans. They seemed to be putting plates on a wide oak table that was at least four trucks long.

"Wait, what's that?" whispered Harry, pointing behind them.

"What?" replied Jack, too mesmerized in looking at the dwarfs place the plates to bother.

"There was something there, like kind of like a black cloud and it felt, sort of evil-like."

"It's probably just your eyes playing tricks on you."

"No, it's not, I'm sure there was something there!" Harry tried to retaliate, but Jack wasn't going to listen, "Anyway, whatever that was, we have to go home, Mom and Dad must be worried about us by now."

"Look!" exclaimed Jack. Some of the dwarf's heads turned towards them and they quickly ducked under their hiding spot.

"Quiet!" whispered Harry.

"But look, they're placing some food on the plates, and, I haven't eaten in days. I'm starving."

"Fine, let's go get some food."

But at that moment a dwarf spotted them.

"Therrrre-a they-a arrre-a" screamed the dwarf, saying 'a' after every word.

"Oh no..." muttered Harry.

"Come-a down-a here my frrriends-a and join-a us for lunch-a," continued the dwarf.

"Should we listen to them?" asked Jack.

"They might know a way to get us back home," replied Harry.

Harry and Jack slowly rose from their hiding spot and calmly walked down into the valley.

Delicious smells wafted up into noses. The dwarfs were placing delicious looking pastries and foods on the plates.

"Umm... hi," said Jack shyly to a dwarf.

"Hello, I am Harry, and this is my brother Jack, we don't know how we got here, and we need a way to get back home," added Harry.

"Yes, yes, that will happen-a and we will tell-a you how-a, but firrrrrst you have-a to eat with-a us," replied the dwarf.

Harry and Jack slowly walked over to the delicious plates. They hadn't realised it but now since they were in front of so much food their stomached grumbled louder than a lion's roar and they remembered they hadn't eaten in days as their mum and dad were poor and they spent most of the time scavenging on the streets for anything they could sell for money or eat. They found some plates and before they knew it their plates were stacked high with delicacies that made their mouths water. They sat on an oak wood table near the buffet and ate next to the dwarf they spoke to earlier.

"Can you tell us how to get home please," asked Jack.

"I don't think I can but maybe Kean will be able to," replied the dwarf.

Out of nowhere, the dwarf Kean appeared with a poof of smoke. He bent down and whispered something to the other dwarf and then looked up at the brothers.

"You need to travel west," he said pointing towards the setting sun.

"It's already 5 pm?" wondered Harry.

"And you will find The Key, once you have that you bring it back to us and we will take you to the door of worlds and from there you will be able to teleport to your world again, Earth, I believe you call it. But the journey will not be easy. You will encounter the shadow of doom and it will try to stop you from..." faltered Kean.

"Sorry, did you say 'shadow' because I saw a black cloud like one earlier!" interrupted Harry.

"Oh no, you must have been brought here for a reason and you must have great power if the shadow is already following you, this makes it even more important for you to leave as if the shadow gets you than you will give it the power to take over the worlds. So, you must leave now!" exclaimed Kean.

"NO NEED FOR THAT!" boomed a voice. It was a swirly black cloud slowly taking the shape of a Minotaur. Its huge chest, body and head were made of a black cloud-like substance, and it didn't have legs. It just had a black cloud under him which he floated on. His horns were pearly white, and his eyes were blood. He flexed his huge muscles and shouted, "I have been waiting for you."

"Go now!" yelled Kean, "I'll try to stop him from coming after you!"

"OH YOU'RE NOT GOING ANYWHERE YOU HUMANS!" bellowed the Shadow of Doom, "THE DARK FAMILY NEEDS YOUR POWER AND THEN WE WILL RISE AGAIN!"

"You can't stop them!" shouted the dwarf who the brothers had spoken to earlier.

The dwarf tossed them two skateboards with no wheels and instead what looked like blue hover pads.

'HOVERBOARD' it read, in bold italic letters on the top. Without thinking the brothers jumped on and flew in to the horizon.

When they reached the place where the dwarfs told them they should go, in front of them was a huge glass dome with a sliding door to enter. The boys couldn't see anyone inside the dome.

They jumped off their hoverboards and carefully placed them behind the tree. They slid silently into the dome and through the door. In the middle of the dome was a glass box on an obsidian pedestal. And inside the box was a golden old-fashioned key with diamonds, rubies and precious stones engraved inside it.

Harry crept towards the box and slowly lifted the glass box. He reached towards the key and tried to grab it, but he just grabbed air.

"Wait, What!" Harry yelped, "It's just a hologram!"

In the blink of an eye, the Shadow of Doom swept down and turned into a black panther with glowing red eyes and a swimming green dot in the middle.

"The Dark Family have retrieved the key before you, this moment has started the revolution of the Dark Lands and we appreciate your help," sneered the Shadow Of Doom.

"How will we ever get home now?" said Jack, terrified....

Hunter and Zoey

by Nandini Ram Mohan

They had always been together, for as long as he could remember. They had always been the best of friends. She had taught him everything he knew, relentlessly preparing him for life in the outside world! This was the moment they had both been waiting for...

Seven years ago...

Zoey, a resourceful, eleven-year-old girl, whose father owned a rehabilitation center for animals, was walking down the surprisingly quiet city lane when she saw some commotion ahead of her on the road.

The first thing she saw was a lion cub who

seemed to have a broken leg. The second thing she saw was people attempting to catch it. And that was what she hated. She immediately sprinted into the commotion and snatched the adorable, innocent lion cub, making a crucial decision to take it to the center and treat it until it got better.

When she got home and asked her dad if she could treat the cub in the rehabilitation center, she was surprised to receive a slight nod as an answer. She dashed across the street to the center, still holding the cub in her hands, ran through the crammed reception, dodging everyone in her way, stopped at the empty enclosures, and set the cub down. At that moment, as he stared into her emerald green eyes, she decided to name him Hunter.

Over the years, the two became extremely close friends, treating each other as siblings.

Zoey devoted almost all of her free time to Hunter, and Hunter responded by playing affectionately with her and obeying her every instruction. Zoey and Hunter were best friends for life.

After four long years of living at the rehabilitation center, Hunter was now a fully-grown adult lion, although both he and Zoey did not realise this. However, Zoey's dad felt that Hunter was becoming too big for the center and had to be relocated. In addition to this, Hunter could become a potential danger in the future, because he was a wild animal, after all.

Hunter was devastated and apprehensive to be taken to the local zoo. Neither Hunter nor Zoey were aware of this, but a few days earlier, Zoey's father had called the zoo and requested them to take Hunter away after he accidentally scratched Zoey's leg while playing in the enclosure with her, injuring her severely. He was also becoming more and more difficult to manage and more expensive to keep as he grew older, another reason why he had to be moved away from the center. The center had limited funds and did not have the money to take care of Hunter and all the animals being rehabilitated there anymore.

The fateful day arrived when the zoo officials came to take Hunter away from Zoey. Somehow, he knew and understood that he would not be seeing his best friend for a long time, if he ever saw her again... He protested as much as possible, even whining and looking pleadingly at Zoey, who was as heartbroken as he was, but she looked away.

Present Day...

Every day, Hunter waited and waited for Zoey to come to the zoo, where he was isolated from any other people except for the visitors who came to gawk at the king of the jungle day in and day out, the people who came to clean his enclosure on a weekly basis, and those who came to feed him. Every day, Zoey waited and waited for Hunter to come back.

A few years passed, and both were convinced that the other had forgotten them. Zoey frequently asked her dad to take her to the zoo where Hunter was. After a lot of persuasion, one day, he relented. Zoey was ecstatic! The zoo where Hunter was being kept was a day's travel away, so Zoey and her father packed their meals for the day and then set off on the long journey.

When they reached the zoo after a long ride, they found out that the lion enclosures were at the very other end of the zoo from where they were. Although they were exhausted and weary, they kept walking and walking until they reached the lion enclosures, knowing that it would be worth it. Hunter, on the other hand, was completing his run-of-the-mill routine. He was about to lie down and go to sleep on the sleek, recently polished and cleaned steel floor of his small and cramped enclosure after another long day of waiting for his friend and having no results whatsoever. He saw a teenage girl who looked about eighteen and her father out of the corner of his eye. Wait... that girl looked familiar... Wasn't that Zoey?

Bewildered, Hunter jumped up and started roaring, scratching and pawing at the glass, doing anything and everything to try and make his beloved old friend Zoey see him. All the visitors and staff around Hunter were astonished to see this as Hunter had always been a very quiet and reserved lion since the time he had entered the zoo.

Zoey was looking at all the lions asleep in their enclosures when she suddenly heard a lion roar from the enclosure opposite the one she was looking at. It was a roar of pure joy.

With tears in her eyes, she made her way up to Hunter's enclosure. "Hunter, is it really you?" Her response was a ground-shaking roar and Zoey's father knew that they had found each other.

Zoey and Hunter both went to sleep that night, content that the other still remembered and loved them.

Zoey, who was now of the age where she could take up an internship as she had finished school, was deciding between two extremely good jobs. In the end, she took the internship where she would be close to her old friend: she took a job at Hunter's zoo!

Both were radiant with joy as they now got to be together for years to come...

A Journey Through Time

by Aarav Dave

Chapter One

As they stood there in the darkness, neither of them could have imagined what would happen next. They found the lantern by chance as they were scouring the streets looking for food. Lying on the cobbled street, waiting to be found, the lantern burnt through the dim light of the evening. The boys held it in their hands, watching the orange flame flicker in the breeze.

Without warning, the flame disappeared, as did the two boys!

When the flame reappeared, the boys could not believe where they were...

Life was non-existent. Destruction and creation were abundant. The sky was a murky black vortex, illuminated only by the weak glow of developing stars. Choppy seas of thick, molten lava strewed the bleak, craggy land, which was encompassed by a range of lofty, ashen mountains. Volcanic geysers dispersed scorching, deadly gases like toxic fountains.

After they slowly opened their eyes, it took Noah and Liam a while to figure out where they were, before coming upon a decision that they were on a forming planet. Hopefully Earth. All was calm, but Liam knew better. They had no food, no water, and he was surprised there was oxygen. Right now, all was well, and his priority was comforting his nine-year-old friend.

"Oh, how barren life is on this planet!" observed Noah as they wandered in search of a way back home. He always used to overlook posters about global warming, and deforestation, and – you get the point. "But," he rationalised, "if this wasteland is the past, is it also our future..." Cutting through his speculations was a thunderous fulmination, a blinding flash, which shook the terrain below their feet. A galactic explosion. Or so he thought. Rocks screamed in every direction, whizzing past their heads. They knew they had to escape but they had nowhere to go. The towering mountains loomed upon them and molten lava just topped it off.

"Agh, that one almost hit me!" yelled Noah over the howling wind.

"Whatever shall we do?" replied Liam. "We have to get out of here – it is escalating, slowly but surely."

"But..." Noah continued, "we're surrounded on all sides; and we don't even know for sure where we are!"

"And we don't have food and water. We must flee sooner than later," said Liam hoarsely. "We should beat a hasty retreat!"

"If there is a way forward, there's always a way back!" exclaimed Noah excitedly, remembering his mother's endless quotes. "And that means, we got here through the lantern –"

"We must get back the same way!" finished Liam breathlessly. They shuffled around to bring the antique lantern into view.

"Maybe we should blow it out?" said Noah. "It disappeared and we came here," he quickly justified looking at Liam's puzzled face. They blew and blew, but it stood on, like a stubborn hippopotamus.

So, the boys had nothing to do, except sit and watch the slowly dying candle illuminate their vicinity – and dodge the unforgiving cannonballs. Little did they know that by doing just this, they were jumping out of the frying pan and into the fire. With one unexpected blow of wind, the flame died out, and rebounded to life somewhere the boys never thought they could be; naturally, with them...

Chapter 2

It took the boys a while for their eyes to adjust to the darkness (even though they had the lantern) before they could comprehend that they were in some kind of a tunnel. As they looked around, they saw a greyish beam of light echoing from one end. A beam of hope. A beam of life. A beam of home.

But as Noah and Liam neared the mouth of the tunnel, all was not as it seemed. They pushed through the colossal clouds of obscure smoke to reveal a blue-grey glimmer. By now, the boys had figured they were in the future. But not the future they had thought it would be. Another lifeless, ruined future. A future which was covered in an overcast of charcoal fumes, and the ground, although the boys couldn't see well, was a chaos of humans, and what seemed like robots. One which had no life, except humans. No nature. No animals. No lush, green fields. Nothing. One where there was nothing to do for anyone, all was autonomous.

As the boys stepped forward into the light, several people approached them offering them refreshments. Although stunned by the fact that they were welcomed this heartily, they walked on, deep in conversation about how the people didn't seem to have any emotions, any feelings. Maybe they were meta-humans?

Noah had still not told Liam about his thoughts before the galactic explosion and was debating whether to do so or not. He eventually came upon the agreement that he would. It was the perfect place and the perfect time.

"Look how..." (he looked for the right word), "...wasted this city is. How destroyed," said Liam.

"I thought I might as well tell you this. While we were in the past on that forming planet thing..." Noah said slowly.

"Yeah," said Liam to show he was listening.

"I was thinking that the past was like a wasteland, and so would our future be the same," continued Noah as they took a turn, "and it is. So, if we don't make a difference now... this is our future."

"I agree," said Liam, "we have to do something. But we can't do anything until we get back. Our priority is getting back. Plus, once we get back nobody will believe our recount."

"Well, yes, but we can persuade them to take care of the planet. But anyhow, we can't get back until the lantern dies out..." before Noah could finish his sentence, the lantern flickered and then died out, and they were whisked back to the uneven, cobbled street. They would never forget their journey through time.

***

The next morning, they started to contemplate how they would influence the world to protect their futures, and hopefully, nobody would have to see the terrorised land they saw.

The Great Adventure of Adam and Zack

by Bissan Kadi

As they stood there silently in the darkness, neither of them could have imagined what would happen next.

They found the lantern by chance as they were scouring the streets looking for food. Lying on the cobbled street, waiting to be found, the lantern burnt through the dim light of evening. The boys held it in their hands, watching the orange flame flicker in the breeze.

Without warning, the flame disappeared, as did the two boys!

When the flame reappeared, the boys could not believe where they were...

"Uh where are we?" questioned Zack.

"I don't know..." answered Adam.

They were sucked into an ebony vortex, teleporting themselves into a one of a kind enchanted forest.

"Uh what now?" asked Adam.

"Blow the candle... maybe the lantern could teleport us back!" shouted Zack.

Suddenly, a boisterous, deep voice informed them that if they don't complete the game they will never leave this mysterious world.

"Game... what game?" asked Adam.

Adam and Zack looked at each other. Before either of them could speak, the voice declared that the game was a simple one. They had to find their way out of the forest before sunset. There would be obstacles and creatures along their path, but if they were brave and determined enough, they could make their way out.

The boys took a deep breath and agreed to the challenge. Armed with nothing but their wits and the lantern, they stepped into the darkness.

The forest was full of secrets and the boys had to be careful. They heard eerie noises coming from the darkness and could feel eyes watching them. Zack was scared but he managed to push his fear aside and continue.

The boys eventually stumbled upon a clearing. In the centre, was a giant tree and Adam realised that the tree was the key to getting out of the forest.

Adam slowly and dramatically touched the key but all of a sudden, the grass beneath them disappeared. They realised that it was a trap. As both of them fell into the abyss, they landed on a small pond in the cave.

"We have to start climbing, the lantern can give us light!" cried Adam.

After a few minutes of climbing, they came across an old door. Zack reached out and opened it to find a small room full of puzzles. He quickly realised that the puzzles were the key to unlocking the door and the way out of the forest.

Adam and Zack spent the next few hours solving the puzzles. They had to think quickly and work together if they were going to make it out. Finally, after much hard work, they were able to solve the last puzzle and unlock the door.

The boys stepped out of the room and were greeted by the most beautiful sight they had ever seen. The sun was setting and the sky was filled with a million stars. In the distance, they could see a bridge and they knew they were free.

As they stood there silently in the darkness, neither of them could have imagined what would happen next...

They had discovered their courage and bravery within the enchanted forest and together they had made it out.

Adam and Zack slowly walked towards the bridge, glancing up at the stars one last time. They knew that they were meant to be here, that they were meant to discover this magical place and they also knew they had to keep it a secret.

After a few moments of admiring the beauty of the setting sun, they began walking back home, the lantern in their hands. They were exhausted but they were sure that the memories of their adventure would remain with them forever.

The two boys made their way through the streets and eventually reached their homes. They said their goodbyes, both of them understanding the magnitude of what had just happened.

Months passed and Adam and Zack did not talk about their experience in the enchanted forest. They both had a feeling that if they did, it would take away from the magic of it all. One day, Adam felt the urge to share their story. He knew that he had to, so he went and found Zack. Without saying a word, he handed him the lantern and together they set off to the forest, determined to share their experience with the world.

Once they arrived, they set up camp and prepared to tell their story. For the next few hours, they narrated their adventure, speaking of the challenges they faced and the courage they had found. When they finished, they knew that they had done justice to the story. They carefully packed up their camp and began the journey back home.

The next morning, word of the boys' incredible journey spread like wildfire.

People from far and wide came to hear their story. Adam and Zack, now heroes of the town, shared with everyone the secrets and wonders of the enchanted forest.

What started as a chance discovery of a lantern on a cobbled street had become a beautiful story of courage, adventure and friendship.

From then on, the boys made sure to visit the enchanted forest every once in a while, and every time they went, they found something new. A new tunnel, a new path, a new puzzle. The forest was full of wonders, and Zack and Adam were determined to uncover all of them.

Their adventures soon became famous and people from all over the world flocked to the enchanted forest to witness the boys' courage and bravery. Adam and Zack were happy to share the stories of their adventures with everyone.

Their journey continued for years, until one day, when Adam and Zack were much older, they decided to call it quits. The lantern was placed in a museum, to be admired by all who visited.

Adam and Zack still talked about their adventures, but now their tales had become more like stories and legends rather than actual events. Nevertheless, the spirit of their journey still lingered in the air, and the enchanted forest still held the same beauty and mystery.

To this day, people still talk about the tale of Adam and Zack, and the incredible journey they took in the enchanted forest. They may have left it long ago, but the spirit of their adventure still lives on...

The Power of Magic

by Honey Ava Gretton

It was my first day at school and I couldn't wait. I stepped outside and stared upwards towards the sun as I saw my hair, as black as coal, fluttering in midair. I smiled: I had never been to school. I'd always been self-taught. Ava, my sister, looked down at me and grinned.

"You ready? Trust me when you get there, you'll regret asking father." She tells me. I rolled my eyes; she hated school. But she had gotten used to it.

"Ready as I'll ever be and it's dad, not father!" I smirk. She makes a slight giggle and continues.

"Father, dad same thing," she shrugs, "just don't get ahead of yourself. I'm still fourteen and you are just ten." She reminds me.

My smirk drops. I get too carried away sometimes and forget my sister's magic is stronger than mine. Oh, I forgot to say! Yeah, our family is made up of wizards. My sister goes to Specking, a school for wizards like secondary or high school. She is a talented witch.

"Hey, are you in there? Are you dreaming again?" I hear my sister talking. I snap back to life once again.

"Oh sorry, I started doing that thing again..." I utter.

"Ugh that thing in your head where you think you are communicating to someone." She scoffs. I turn my head away.

"Yeah... let's just get in the ca.. what is it again?" I ask. She scrunches her face.

"Car. It's a car. You can't be like this in front of normies," she states strictly.

"Just get in and let's get on the road," she commands me.

"Ok then..." I whisper and get in. I take one glance at the house and turn to go into the car.

I stand at the front of the school with unease. My sister had already been laughing at my choice of school outside the house. Shivers went up and down from my head to my toes as I neared the school gate. But I knew deep in my heart that I would never leave my house if I remained homeschooled. I carefully stepped into the building.

"What the..." I whisper. A bunch of girls are in the hallway doing a weird dance.

"It must be a human ritual!" I realise after moments of confusion. I shake my head and walk to a skinny cupboard; my name is scrapped into position on its door. OOF! I fell to the ground with a giant thud!

"Ow, oops I'm so sorry!" A kid rolls off me in fear and horror.

"It's fine but do you mind explaining why you ran into me?" I mutter, rising from the cold marble floor with a sliver of annoyance.

"Oh I'm sorry I was running away from Jack.." the boy mutters. I frown.

"Who's Jack and why were you running from him?" I asked with curiosity.

"He's the school bully, you don't know him? Ohhh wait you must be new, yeah? We were told yesterday we'd have someone new! That must be why you don't know him! Anyway, I'm Biffle and I'm eleven, what about you?" he asks me not leaving a moment for himself to breathe.

"I'm River and I'm ten but what do you mean why do I not know him?" I ask.

He stares at the ground in sadness, almost fretting to tell me about him behind his back.

"I'll tell you but not here," Biffle tells me.

"Well, I should show you around before class starts," he explains to me. I agree and he starts to show me around.

The class ends and we head out. Biffle had shown me around and now I was growing tired.

"Being at a school outside home is confusing," I mutter. Biffle stares at me oddly.

"What do you mean by that, were you homeschooled?" Biffle asked me. I nod as we continue to walk down the hallway. I avert my gaze to look at an anti-bullying sign.

"Speaking of which, do you mind telling me about that.. Uh... what's his name again?" I asked him curiously. My bones shake uncontrollably with fear, with uncertainty.

"Oh... you mean Jack? Yeah, he bullies teachers as well as students. I got a bit angry with him a while back and that's how I ran into you because I..I. I tried to prank Jake and he got really mad so I had to run," he explains struggling to push each word out of his mouth. We turned a corner and I see a teacher with wet hair that was dropping down to his eyes.

"Oh no... It's him," Biffle sighs. I attempted to ignore the large teacher that looked like a giant standing in front of me, but he wasn't letting me go past him.

"What do you need teacher?" I scoff at the man. My friend stamps on my feet. His foot felt like an elephant!

"Teacher!? Get out of my way idiot! I'm not a puny teacher! I'm here for Biffle not you!" he exclaims. My brain sends a ghost to go and haunt every inch of my body.

"No! Please forgive me I was forced!" Biffle cries falling to the floor. I gasped. It was Jack.

"You liar, you have disrespected me for the last time and now you will face the consequences!" Jack yells picking Biffle up from his shirts collar. Anger fills the course of my blood heading all the way to my heart, filling it with immense hatred.

"DROP HIM!" I shriek. My sadness and wrath battling for control over the still sane parts of my soul. Jack laughs and raising him in the air, he drops Biffle with the power of Zeus within the core of his hands. This was the last straw...

"You mess with the bull you get the horn!" he laughs at Biffle as blood trembles out his mouth: he was speechless. A kid comes out from behind the corner cheering on Jack quietly, entirely with fear for his own safety instead of my friends. I raise my hand aiming it at Jack with intense aim.

"Indeed, but this bull doesn't need horns to mess around," I chuckle. He turns around and stretches his eyes.

"What are you doing?" he asks, rolling his eyes mockingly. I giggle and he moves into position to prepare for the worst.

"This, Estimos caprada!" I cry focusing my brain on the cruel boy in front of me. The effects took a matter of mini seconds but when it was processed the boy floated in the unforgiving air with a whip from the air I was controlling.

"What is happening!" he exclaims.

"This!" I laugh spinning him around in the air until throwing him down with all my power down the school stairs. Dropping my hand down in exhaustion, I stared upwards from my position on one knee. Every kid was staring at me. I widened my eyes petrified; my parents had only let me go to normal school on the promise nobody would find out about my secret. But to my surprise, they started clapping! The normies actually started clapping!

"Are you a.. a wizard?" Biffle asks, running over to me as fast as his legs could move. I nod.

To my complete disbelief, everyone looked at me in awe. In amazement. In admiration! Even those weird human rituals had stopped to watch my magic and what I had done. For years, my parents had warned me to hide my powers from the world. Now, I am wondering why? If my magic can be used for good, this is exactly what I will do.

I guess for now I just need to say one thing. Never underestimate those around you. You never know when there might be a Wizard ready to put a bully in their place!

If you can be one thing, be kind. Which I hope my sister will be when she finds out about this!

The Amazing Adventures of
Emma and Jackson

by Celena Bou Habib

"Look! Look down there!" His voice could just about be heard above the sound of the aeroplane's engine and the shrieking wind in their ears.

"Can you see it?"

Chapter 1: Thunder's Coming

Twenty-four hours before...

As the golden sun rose, the mischievous duo, Emma and Jackson, made their way towards what Jackson called 'his nightmare.' Jackson resented school. Every second ticking by was another second of enduring misery and pain. His twin, on the other hand, was the complete opposite. "It's not that bad; you'll make friends soon, I just know it!" She would loquaciously ramble on.

"Yeah, yeah," grumbled Jackson groggily.

As time crept by, the indefinite school day eventually came to an end, as did eventually Jack's foul mood.

"Still no luck with the friends thing?" asked Emma half-heartedly. After all, she did ask this question seven days a week.

Jackson paused. "Err, no, not really," he shrugged.

Before Emma could mutter a word, a swirling haze of roars could be heard from not too far away.

"What was that?" she trembled, her eyes rolling out of their sockets. SWOOSH! It thundered, like a train storming down a track.

"A...is it a...thunderstorm?" stammered back her brother.

Continuous puffs of air wheezed by, leaving the twins quaking in their shoes. Hastily, bombastic, barbaric gusts of wind blew them off their feet! But this was not just wind.

Struck with disbelief, the pair exchanged alarmed glances to find themselves strapped against a plane's wing! Booming cries of help, the aghast children bawled their eyes out, wept until they could no more, and slowly drifted off into an abyss of numbness.

Beaming down on the twins, a mellow rush of air settled upon the sky. Groaning into a stretch, the frazzled pair made sense of their surroundings, rapidly jolting awake. The engine spluttered deafening gasps of air, piercing their ears and whirling their hair through the sky, leaving their stomachs churning with fright.

"How are we going to make it back home?" shrieked Emma. "Will we ever see our parents again? Will we ever sleep in our beds again? Will we ever live normal lives? Will we ever..."

Jackson plastered his hand against her mouth—he didn't want to endure the peppering of the endless pesters. "Will you ever shut up?" he huffed, but he couldn't mask the terror seizing his throat.

"What's that?" Emma squinted, peering down at the cloak of murkiness beneath her.

"Huh? What's what?" came back her brother's puzzled voice.

"Over there! Can you see it?" she squealed.

Chapter 2:   Otium City, The Land of Fun

Screeching to a halt, the plane landed in a decreasingly realistic area, teeming with hordes of feisty children. Strikingly exotic creatures roamed around a place so magical it did not seem real. The pair exchanged glances of utter confusion as they gawked at the bewildering sights unfolding in front of them. All of a sudden, a tall, thin woman with an elegant figure greeted them. She spoke with a thick British accent and was surprisingly the only person there who had acknowledged the twins.

"Hello, my name is Rebecca. I'm sure you're wondering why you're here. Well, I'll take you to someone who has all the answers." She led them towards a monumental tower that stood so high the top was hidden by the blanket of clouds! After a boundless journey of blood, sweat, and tears, the three finally made it to the top of the tower.

Stumbling into a chasm of gloom, the pair gasped for air as they gaped at Rebecca, who stood unfazed. Adjusting their eyes to the darkness, Emma and Jackson craned their necks to get a view of the entire room, just to find that it was an empty space, drained of any source of bliss.

"This is the land of fun!" boomed a blaring, thunderous voice, sending shivers down their spines. The pair shared a frazzled glance. "Anything you wish for here will come true, and you have been chosen to stay!"

"But we don't want to stay here! We want to go back home!" shrieked Emma, her voice breaking. Deafening silence hung in the room.

"You may," growled back the raspy, hoarse voice. The pair's eyes lit up. "Under one condition! You two must capture the masked darkener!"

"The masked what?" asked Jackson, muddled.

"An anonymous figure has been casting repulsive spells upon our land of joy, and you two must stop this!"

And so the twins made a deal.

Chapter 3: The Vicious Venture

The scorching sun sizzled over Otium City, seeping into the windows across the diamond of dreams.

"Well, we better get to work!" Emma exclaimed; a grin plastered onto her face.

Woozy moans came back from her brother, who lay vegging on a tremendously oversized couch. Rubbing his bleary eyes, he gazed at the rosy hue that shimmered along the morning sky. Dragging her brother out of his state of relaxation, they set out to find the masked darkener! The land brought them many shocks as they fought through their adventure. Spewing lava chased them along mountains, animals of all kinds sauntered about, and they had numerous encounters with strange people.

Hours passed by, and the pair sought out every inch of the land in hope of seeking the enemy. They kept their eyes peeled for anything that would lead them to the figure, but soon after, any glimpses of hope were lost. As the sky was lit ablaze by the fire of the setting sun, it cast long shadows onto the ground. The pair admired the golden drops of the sunset, which gave a warm, orange tinge to the sky.

"It's getting dark; we should head back," yawned Emma, her eyes drooping. With dusk draping down on them, they trudged sluggishly back to their room.

Bundled up in their beds, Emma and Jackson dozed off into slumbers when, all of a sudden, the lights began to flicker, and their front door burst open. Not daring to breathe, the pair shared glances of pure dread as their heads pounded and their stomachs churned. The floorboards creaked as the noise neared, and an anonymous silhouette swiftly barged through their room! The masked darkener! The pair lurched out of their beds, hurtling any objects in sight at the figure. Abruptly, the silhouette rapidly fired darts at the twins as they ricochet off surfaces, missing their heads by a hair. They needed to think, and fast! Snatching the bedsheet off the bed, Emma hurled the sheets at the figure, slowing it down. Briskly, Jackson charged at the silhouette, chucking the mask off.

"Rebecca?" spluttered the twins in unison, looks of bemusement cast upon their faces. "Ugh, you caught me!" she whined. With Rebecca strapped to a chair, the pair took her all the way to the tower, ready to be sent home.

Chapter 4:   Home Sweet Home

The night sky was aglow with city lights as Emma and Jackson lay on the grass, gazing at the blanket of stars that stretched to infinity. "We sure have many adventures together," chuckled Jackson.

"We sure do, and we always will, for years to come!" replied Emma, peering at the pale crescent moon that shone like a silvery claw in the night sky. The scene was both eerie and ethereal in equal measure.

"I had a really fun time with you," smiled Jackson, with hints of sincerity in his tone.

"Same," beamed Emma, a twinkle glistening in her eye.

Nothing but silence echoed through the night, with the occasional barking of the faraway dogs, but the twins didn't sleep, they didn't bat an eye, they only thought to themselves, "What an amazing adventure!"

A Bedtime Tale

by Kiara Jain

As they stood silently in the darkness, neither of them could have imagined what would happen next. They found the lantern by chance as they were scrounging the street for food.

Lying on the cobbled street, waiting to be found, the lantern burnt through the dim light of evening. The boys held it in their hands, watching the orange flame flicker in the breeze.

Without warning, the flame disappeared, as did the two boys.

When the flame reappeared, the boys could not believe where they were...

They stood up and brushed off their red and white checked, grubby t-shirts, which hung limply around their underfed stomachs and pale skin. Their dark, chocolate brown hair had become home to a variety of different insects and long greasy strands dangled helplessly over their ice blue eyes, which were fixed on their surroundings. They noticed everything seemed magical, yet unusually familiar. It was like when a piece of information is just out of reach.

In the blink of an eye it snapped, they were not just hearing someone read Goldilocks out loud to them, they were inside the story. The aroma of freshly made, sugary, sweet-smelling porridge filled the air and the feeling of warmth and comfort engulfed them. Memories, long concealed, came flooding back like a river after torrential downpour. They remembered their parents tucking them into bed with a bed-time story. Begging to be read to one more time.

So, as Goldilocks tumbled down from the baby bear's petite chair, only a hickory brown, wooden floor - which wore a threadbare, crimson and mahogany, striped carpet - the boys could not help but feel a part of their memories return.

Before they could open their mouths, darkness pounced on them from all directions, leaving them with nothing but heart-breaking memories left to tear them apart from the inside. So they stood there in silence; their filthy nails clinging onto each other's and their breath as ragged as their clothes.

The devastating, catastrophic, earthquake, which had taken place nearly three grueling months ago still haunted their deepest, darkest memories. Terrified civilians screaming, trying to get out of the crumbling, caving building as fast as possible. Mum running in the way of a large, heavy chandelier, which promptly fell on her. Dad was being pushed off the small, unstable balcony in the midst of the chaos. The twins themselves had escaped seconds before the place they had once called their home exploded into a roaring blaze of crackling fire leaving nothing in its wake but ash and smoking hot coals of glowing embers.

Suddenly, the setting around them changed again. Long, thick strands of mist covered the grass that crunched underfoot. Lush, emerald, green pine trees with ancient, burnt-sienna brown bark surrounded them and a majestic, beautiful stag with large, curved antlers stood drinking from a nearby stream, which flowed with cool crystalline water. There was a heavenly aroma of an assortment of sugary goodies, coming from the right. A loud rustle of bushes covered in large, juicy strawberries scared the boys out of their wits but when they recognized Hansel and his twin sister Gretel they laughed, a thing they did not do very often these days. In fact, neither boy could remember the last time they had smiled...

A swell of warmth erupted inside their hearts as another part of them slotted back into place. They recalled the rough last months and realised that these imaginary friends had kept them going. They both burst into a round of laughter for no apparent reason but kept on laughing until it felty like the weight of the world had been lifted off their shoulders and they were a feather hovering in the air without a care in the world. Before they knew what was happening their feet lifted off the ground and were hovering several meters above where Hansel and Gretel were standing near the stream.

"Hansel do you smell that?" Gretel asked, sniffing the air around her.

"I don't know what that is but it smells.."
POP!

That's all the twins heard of that conversation before there was a noise like a bubble bursting and their little invisible cocoon vanished into this air and it sent the boys tumbling to the ground. Just before the rocks would have beaten them to pulp the walls folded in and the next thing, they knew they landed on a layer of freshly watered, overgrown grass littered with beautiful buttercups and delicate daisies next to a large, sturdy oak tree, which looked as if it has been there for centuries. The inconvenient landing jolted the air out of their lungs.

Although this time they recognised the story immediately.

"Snow White and the seven dwarfs!" they cried in unison. Emotion welled behind their eyes as they saw their childhood companions and the stories that had put them to sleep for many nights came alive before them. All that could be seen of the stunning ball of fire on the horizon went down. They found the lantern by chance as they were searching for something to satisfy the growling of their starved stomachs. Lying under the tree the ancient oak waiting to be found. The lantern burnt through the gloom of the night, the flame flickering in the chilly august air. The boys used it to warm their bitter arms, absentmindedly watching the glowing light of their mind racing through all the day's new discoveries.

Without warning, the flame disappeared as did the two boys. When the flame reappeared, the boys were back on the cobbled streets but their hearts radiating with a glow of warmth fueled by memories but most of all by friendship.

Future and I

by Kunal Sethia

I moved to Japan last summer, and besides crazy Pokemon fans, what I saw made me marvel at this country more than I ever have done. Cherry blossoms surrounded our house. The sky-high mountains towered over us as the white clouds sparkled like jewels. All this was a speck compared to everything else Japan could show off. Among mountains, trees, and forests, Japan also had a large culture for anime, manga, idols, and video games. Japan has created an impressive number of famous arts and shows we know today.

It was cold, but with a jacket, a stroll through the forest with my dog, Future, would be incredible. A German Shepherd, Future, was big and muscular, but lovable the same. We are inseparable. As we exited our house, I decided that we could do this walk every day. The sights were truly breath-taking. The slow wind brushed off a couple of the bright, pink leaves that belonged to the cherry blossoms. We walked down a trail of hard mud which ended at a waterfall. It was quite tall, but Future and I could climb the rocks.

After what felt like hours, we made it to the top. We continued walking until Future started yelping. I rushed over to where he was, confused as to what he had sniffed out. What I saw made me gasp. A sizeable gemstone glittered in the ground! I picked it up, polished my glasses, and dusted off the mud covering it. I exclaimed loudly in excitement. It was as large as my palm, and it had lots of vibrant and dark colours. I was awestruck with amazement. I grabbed the stone and started sprinting home as fast as I could, Future scampering behind me. I told my parents everything. My dad immediately called the police and handed over the stone to them.

After a couple of days, my dad received a call from the Government department. It was then explained to us that the stone we found had been lost decades ago. It was robbed from the palace of the late Emperor Akihito, and it seemed that the thief found it too risky to keep it with him or sell it, so he hid the stone in the forest! And Future found it!

We were invited to Emperor Naruhito's palace. The next morning, a Rolls Royce came to pick us up, and we reached the emperor's palace in an hour. It was one of the most opulent buildings I had ever seen!

As I entered, we got to see mounds of gleaming, giant gold nuggets, oil paintings, and red velvet carpets! That day was due to be a proud occasion. The palace staff greeted us warmly and guided us to the emperor's private chambers. Emperor Naruhito welcomed and thanked us for finding the priceless stone that had been passed down for generations in his family. He rewarded us handsomely.

The next day, my meeting with the emperor was featured on the front page of the local newspaper! Future and I had become famous! The emperor threw a massive party in our honour. Wherever I went people recognised him and me. My life had flipped around in a heartbeat. For the next couple of months, we had become celebrities.

However, on one fateful night, as I twisted and turned in bed, I heard howling. Drowsily, I got up and stumbled down the stairs, falling off the last two. As I swayed and stood up, I saw a shadow through the window. I opened the door and Future ran to me, barking and whimpering noisily. It seemed like he had sensed something. He wouldn't stop barking! I decided to go to my dad's laboratory, where he conducts experiments as a geologist. He agreed and rushed and fetched his car keys, put Future in the back seat, and zoomed away into the distance within seconds.

After a few minutes, I reached my dad's laboratory and he immediately got to work, rummaging through stacks of papers, all filled with scientific notes. He finally found one related to animals' senses. He took out a heavy leather-bound book, inserted a key into it, and showed me the 10th page. It showed how the irrational behaviour of some species of animals can sense disaster about to occur. Signs of the late-night barking and sudden, unprovoked tension proved this.

My dad logged into his computer and used his seismometer, which converts the vibrations given out by earthquakes into electrical signals that can be displayed on a screen.

Thus, giving the user the exact specifications of the size, timing, and distance of the earthquake. This is like how animals use echolocation. The sound they emit travels through the air and bounces back off whatever it hits, helping the animal determine the size, direction, and distance of the prey from its current location. His studies proved that abnormal moments of the tectonic plates would cause an earthquake, a tsunami, or both in the region around Fukushima in the next 48 hours. Fukushima was a city in Japan around 284 km from where I was. I panicked. Taking my dad along, we drove to the Emperor's palace.

Sadly, I couldn't just enter the palace. I explained the situation to the numerous guards surrounding the palace. I told the guards all about it, praying they would believe us.

Unfortunately, that was not the case. I sighed. What kind of a choice did we have?

There was no chance they would ever let us in. Suddenly, the door opened, and out walked Emperor Naruhito. He was given a detailed description of us and instantly recognised us for retrieving his precious gemstone. He knew we did not come to dilly-dally. We were serious. He allowed us in, and my dad showed him all his research and results from the seismometer, concluding what was about to happen. Emperor Naruhito listened carefully and intently, realising we were correct. He sent out a request for everyone in the town to evacuate.

In a day, the city was empty and deserted. Not a single soul was present. The research team, containing twelve people, were eagerly pushing their scrawny noses into the computer screen, which is connected to the city cameras, waiting for something to happen. Then they saw it. A massive tidal wave the size of thirty elephants stacked on top of each other charged at the city.

A matter of minutes before the whale of a wave hit the city, the ground started rumbling.

The researchers were awestruck. They had never seen anything like it. Then I noticed something. Something that made my blood run cold. There was a large nuclear power plant about to collapse! But it was too late. The tower creaked and smashed into the ground. Substantial amounts of radioactive gas hissed and escaped the chamber, leaving behind a trail of green, slimy radioactive waste. I was in shock at the smouldering destruction of the city. It lasted for hours, but the radiation was so strong that the city had become inhabitable for days. Plus, the piles of rubble which were once roads and homes were dangerous and not an ideal place to live in. Civilians struggled to survive underground, and children yearned to go play outside. Though everyone was worried sick about their homes, belongings, and other items, they were grateful to be alive.

The government was grateful to my dad, me, and Future. We had rescued an entire city from losing its population. I tried not to think about what would have happened if Future did not raise his warning call, but the thought always made me shudder. The Emperor was so thankful we had saved the city just in time. My dad and I were rewarded, and we were known as heroes throughout the land once again, with Future being the centre of the talk.

One dog had saved hundreds of thousands of people. The aftermath was that Japan survived.

Stories

by

- Secondary -

Ryaan Saad Abdalla

Hadi Marji

Zaina Tariq

George Bou Habib

The Perfect Girl?

by Ryaan Saad Abdalla

I guess you could say that she was an old friend. She wasn't just a friend to me, she was the girl I fell in love with. The girl, for which I would kill. The girl for which I would die. The girl that I loved but would never love me back.

Her hair was shiny but not blinding, her eyes were consuming yet welcoming, her fragrance was strong but not overwhelming. I had fallen before her before I had even known her name. She was the girl that I had always pictured, the princess yet to meet her prince charming. To this day I still remember the first words you spoke to me, the first conversation we had. Your sweetness, it still rings in my mind as I sleep. I wait for the day that I get to relive that moment, to experience that high again, to be swept off my feet into a frenzy of gratitude to finally see you again. Radiating, you walked through the bookstore door and there I knew you were the one.

I had to know that an ill-mind was covered by your kindness and beauty; I had to know that you weren't one of those fiends that plague the modern day with their lies and facades. Your life was fascinating yet humble, you were busy yet still found the time to be with friends. You were all I could ever ask for and all I had to do was muster the courage to make my move.

The perfect girl.

To this day, I use your advice and I will never forget the things that you told me. I will never forget that love is only a matter of right time and right place. Love is luck.

And I was lucky.

On a late Friday night, I began to give in and give up on trying to find you, a needle in a hay pit. A girl in a city of twelve million people. It was impossible. A lost cause. But that day I was blessed, unfortunately by your misfortune and sadness, but I saw you again.

Stumbling, you soullessly limped down the subway steps with rivers flowing from your eyes. All I wanted to do was hug you and never let go, to let you be forever content. I had to play it cool, I had to be the careless guy that all the girls crave, but I couldn't. I could not see you like that. I ran to you as quickly as possible, with a smile that was amicable but not too amicable. I just wanted to help, to make you feel better. I wanted to kill whoever made you feel that way, but I just had to listen and understand first.

Stuttering, you blurted out who it was, the Satan that had made you feel this way. It was your shameful excuse for a boyfriend, lying and manipulating you constantly and yet you still stayed through the undeserved pain. I had to fix it. I had to make you happy. I knew what I had to do. But before I did it, I had to make sure you were safe.

I never realized the effect that you would have on me, the constant want to be next to you, the constant need for your touch and affection. It was a feeling I had always wanted but never had. All I had to do was to eradicate that pest that somehow turned your head and then I could finally make my wants realities. If only I knew how to lure him in, to take advantage of his weakness and his thick, rumor-filled, social media controlled conscience.

I could only thank you for this part, it was your advice that I still follow to this day.

"If you don't get caught, you did not do anything wrong."

Out of your mouth, these words sounded wise

and harmless, out of anybody else I would see it as despicable and malicious. You. You had a way of sugarcoating everything, I had seen you once after the subway and yet I could already feel myself coming out when I was around your beauty and deafening smile. You could have been describing a murder and still bounce up and down excitedly and giggle every few words. You just never saw any dreadfulness in the world and all I wanted was to be there next to you through that happiness and unique societal outlook. He had to disappear. He had to, you were attached, too much for your own good.

I had to protect you. You told me you would do anything for somebody you love and to this day I live with your words on repeat in my mind. A drug stopping the guilt from taking over. The guilt of protecting you. I loved you so I could do whatever was needed to keep you safe.

Right?

I lured him in with a business deal, an opportunity from him to kickstart the useless idea he had. I lured him into a blow with a hammer. I lured him into inevitable death. But it was for love. Right?

I panicked, I had been overcome by your charm. I had become vindictive for a maybe. For a chance to by the man you wake up to every night. I had killed just to give myself better odds of being your friend. I may have learned some lessons from you but not all of them were things to do, lots were things to not.

I had done it. I held the hammer. I struck him in the head. Nobody else. No way to divert the blame. Before I could get back to relentlessly try and make my dream a reality, I had to deal with the whining pest sitting tied up at the bottom of my store. You couldn't know he was gone, but you couldn't miss him. I had to play my cards right to finally have a chance at being the man cooking breakfast for you in the morning. The man bringing you a cup of tea after a hard day of work.

I had to fill in as your scumbag boyfriend for a little while. All while trying to make you mine. I was living two lives, I had to be myself and yet be him. I had to be him yet still be myself for you. You taught me to never chase a girl like you. A girl who doesn't know what she wants. It's a hassle.

I wanted you so badly. I needed you. I had to get rid of him so I could only focus on you. So I actually had a chance to win you over. Not always having to look over my shoulder wondering if he escaped. I had to kill him. But it was for love. Right?

You also taught me to keep things close to my chest. Told me to be a private person. If only it was easier on my conscience following what I did. I'm inches away every day from blurting out my sin just to relieve the weight on my heart. I did it all for you.

And you still couldn't love me.

After I dealt with him, I moved my focus to you. To your luscious blonde hair and aquamarine eyes. I tried to be your perfect man. I tried to be your biggest supporter. I did everything I could to have the chance at being your other half. It took time. It took changing myself for the worse. It took me accepting your fatal flaws, flaws that would bring me crashing down in the future. But in the end I became your man, I made you breakfast and I kissed you goodbye in the morning. I did everything for you. I suffered through outings with your self-centered friends. I stayed home alone when you went to deal with one of their ridiculous meltdowns about a petty insult. I was so sick of the mental baggage that came with being around you. But I stayed for love, right?

I stuck with you through your ups and downs, always being the shoulder for you to cry on. Always agreeing and never opening your eyes to reality. My love had left me numb, unable to see the truth and the toxicity you brought to my life. I stuck through it all because I loved you, because a girl as pretty and loving as you could never be evil. A girl like you could never be unhealthy for me. Right?

I did everything and yet you could never tell me that you loved me. I had to get out and that's what I did.

I gained nothing from you, but I learnt one thing from you:

"Some people just aren't worthy of love."

An Undying Friendship

by Hadi Marji

As the flame re-appeared the friends found themselves in a magical forest. It was so majestic and so enchanting that one would think they were in the dreams of an angel. Fragrant and leafy trees stood tall, some reaching heights only reached by skyscrapers.

The smell of this wondrous forest alone would bewitch even the devil himself. Gentle breezes of wind brushed off the petals of delicate roses that nourished the forest. As serene birds soared with the wind and beautified the land with their echoing song plants of all sorts flowered and animals from a fox with fur the colour of rubies to peacocks with an iridescent complexion of colours. The friends gazed around with wonder and fascination. Their names are Adam and Maxwell. Adam was a man always seeking adventure and will demolish any foe that approaches him. He was an immature 25-year-old but had the kindest heart. He was great friends with Maxwell since they met (running away from some people they despise) Maxwell was an intelligent and rational person, he was twenty three years old and he would love to recite the first 1500 digits of pi. they both possessed magical powers and an enchanted flame that they have kept running in a lantern for this flame can transport them through space and time. They found it once as they were hiking in an unknown mountain.

"Curious?" Maxwell pondered. "I wonder where the flame has taken us this time?"

Adam was too starstruck to answer the question. He gazed at the forest like a blind person being able to see for the first time.

"I can't believe it." Adam began. "This is no ordinary forest. It's magic; I can feel it."

Just as the friend started into the forest, they saw a darkness pass over them. This usually wouldn't be worrying but the sky was clear and not a single cloud hovered above them.

Maxwell and Adam felt a chill creep down their spines. Darkness enveloped the land like a blanket for as far as they can. Not only had the light vanished but the darkness seemed to shrouded their happiness with grief. The whole sky was blocked by what appeared to be a giant. Within the blink of an eye, the sky was back to normal although the friends felt uneasy. Little did they know what was coming for them...

It had been three hours since the friends had arrived at what they thought was a wonderful, peaceful and harmonious place, and darkness had fallen. As the moon illuminated in the ebony sky the boys were shivering from the cold and they couldn't find the lamp, therefore, they could not go back to their home. The friends were cold, starving, exhausted and thirsty. Suddenly, they felt a strong gush of wind smash into them. It was an unusual wind. They felt it not on their skin but in their hearts. It was a wind that gave them a very uneasy and distraught feeling. All of a sudden, Adam fell to the ground of the fields and Maxwell tried to awaken him.

"Adam, are you ok?" Maxwell yelled but he didn't respond.

Suddenly, Maxwell had a vision. This was not rare as he had regular visions but this one was very unusual. It wasn't a vision of the future, but a vision of the past. Or so it seemed. He was in what seemed to be a memory, but it was twisted and sinister. The said vision displayed him meeting Adam for the first time. Unlike the true way he met Adam (which was while running away from some people he hated back in school); Adam was the villain and it seemed he was trying to injure Maxwell. He suddenly snapped out of the vision and found himself on the floor with tears crippling down his cheeks. His fingers were numb, and his body was shivering but he knew he had to endeavor. He stood up and he had to carry his now half-awake friend to a small cave he saw, and they spent the rest of the night there.

As the friends awoke, they found themselves not in their promised sunrise but chained to a wall in a pitch-black room. It took the two a moment to realise what situation they were in. The uneasy feeling of fear and dread had gushed through them like a river. They had waited some time in the humid room when they heard the door unlocked and the huge iron door opened. A large man wearing a black mast holding an axe entered the room. As tension filled the air, a woman wearing an elegant rose-gold tiara and a white cotton and sheer gown gracefully entered the room. The utter beauty of this woman was no match for the room. In confusion, they quickly began questioning what was going on.

"Who are you?" Adam began.

"Why are we here?" questioned Maxwell.

"You know who we are and why you are here," the women began, "if you do not then I shall inform you. I am Queen Angena from the Moralesubima family. I rule over the Kingdome of Semoran. You have been charged with multiple counts of murder, arson, cannibalism, and theft. We found the stolen items in the cave you were sleeping in. We are required to execute you. You killed my father and so I will kill you and the next seven generations of your family! The only reason I am not publicly burning you at the stake is because the slots are all being used so instead, I will behead you here."

A feeling of grief, dread and anxiety settled in their stomachs when suddenly Maxwell lost consciousness and had another vision. He was on one of his trips with Adam. They were exploring Atlantis before it sunk but instead of attempting to save Atlantis from sinking like in reality, Maxwell and Adam were trying to drown each other in the underwater Atlantis.

Maxwell suddenly woke up and at that moment he began to become corrupt and had the intensions of killing his dear friend Adam. As he re-opened his eyes, he was well again but he saw Adam on the floor with beads of sweat trickling down his forehead and his eyes tearing up as the executor was preparing for the execution.

Suddenly, Maxwell's eyes shone a bright light and he had a small flame emerging from his chest. The flame engulfed the room and in the blink of an eye they were back on the streets.

"Adam! I am so glad you are ok!" exclaimed Maxwell.

Just when they thought that everything was ok the queen re-appeared.

"Well, hello," she sneered.

"I see you have a magical flame. I used to have one too. That is how I got to the Kingdom, killed the King, and became Queen. I wore my flame out so I am going to need yours."

"We will never give it to you!" cried the boys.

"Then I will take it!"

A flame suddenly flew out of her hand and hit Maxwell in the chest as he fell to the ground. The queen began extracting the flame from Adams soul. Adam slowly levitated as she took the flame emerging from his chest, but he was finding it hard to breathe. Suddenly, Maxwells eyes lit up again and he fired icicles at the Queen, and it struck her in the chest. Blood was gushing out of her, and she was slowly but surely dying. The Queen had a hail of icicles piercing her back as she lay face down on the blood-soaked floor.

Maxwell returned to normal, and he finally acknowledged the fact that they both have elemental powers. The queen began freezing and turning into ice when she finally shatters into hundreds of pieces. Adam and Maxwell ran off until they finally reached their apartment.

"What a trip?" Adam declared.

"I know, right?" Maxwell said when suddenly he collapsed to the floor.

Maxwell had yet another corrupted vision. In this one, Adam was running away from Maxwell, who had a knife. When Maxwell woke up his eyes were red with fury, and he began to charge at Adam. Maxwell raced into the cramped kitchen and tightly gripped a razor sharp knife. He had begun chasing Adam around their apartment until he pinned him to the wall making him fear for his life. A sudden overwhelming sensation of agony and melancholy engulfed Adam in this moment

"Maxwell! What are you doing?!" questioned Adam with fear.

Maxwell suddenly snapped out of his trance and admitted to Adam the visions he had been experiencing. He suddenly had the urge to tear him limb by limb once more and continuously attack him relentlessly.

"Max!" yelled Adam, "don't you remember. We always had the best of times together. Don't you remember how we met? We were pranking our enemies. Please Max. Remember."

Max suddenly fell in a trance again and fell to the floor but instead of having a negative vision, as he had usually had, he began to remember things for how they used to be.

Adams visions were gone and Adam forgave him as time went by. In the end, Maxwell and Adam spent the rest of their lives together.

There were many ups and downs but the friend will have an archive of everlasting memories and an unbreakable bond never seen before. Although they had many lows in their lives, that was surely not their last adventure...

Old Friends Stay Together

by Zaina Tariq

As they stood there silently in the darkness, neither of them could have imagined what would happen next. They found the lantern by chance as they were scouring the streets looking for food. Lying on the cobbled street, waiting to be found, the lantern burnt through the dim light of evening. The boys held it in their hands, watching the orange flame flicker in the breeze. Without warning, the flame disappeared, as did the two boys! When the flame reappeared, the boys could not believe where they were.

"River, where are we?" Leo asked in a hushed voice, his eyes filled with curiosity. Leo was the shorter boy of the two, with dirty blonde hair and large brown eyes. Beside him was his best friend, River. River was only a few centimeters taller than Leo, he was brunette and had piercing green eyes. They were in a large room with white walls, which were decorated with beautifully detailed paintings and gorgeous golden furniture. There were three windows on one of the walls, all of which stretched from the floor to the ceiling.

"I'm not sure," River started, "but it's nice and warm here. It beats being outside."

The boy shrugged off his oversized coat, sighing contently when the warm air hit his exposed arms. Leo mimicked this and started wandering towards the windows. He listened to the soft pitter-patter of the raindrops hitting the glass from outside, until a low grumble from his stomach tore through the silence of the place.

"So, you're hungry, too," River observed.

Leo nodded, as his hand hovered over his hollow stomach. "Do you think there's food around?"

"There's got to be," Leo started, then nodded towards a pair of wooden doors on the wall behind his friend. The doors stretched from the floor to the ceiling and looked very heavy. "Why don't we go check?"

Together, they stalked towards the doors. Leo wrapped his finger around one of the handles, whilst River did the same on the other.

"1,2,3," River muttered, and they both used all the strength they could muster to push the doors open.

Behind both doors was a long, silent hallway. The floors were made of marble, and so were the walls. There were many gold-framed paintings scattered across the walls, all of which were portraits of unfamiliar people.

After waiting for a few seconds, River cautiously started walking forward with Leo following suit. The sounds of their gentle footsteps echoed off the walls, as they kept on going until two new hallways appeared, one on each side.

"Which way?" Leo whispered, as if raising his voice would cause the entire building to come crashing to the ground.

River hesitated, then nodded towards the hallway on the left. It was only a few meters long, with a pair of similar wooden doors at the end. They pushed them open together, and the smell of food instantly hit them. It was a mixture of meat, cheeses, and fresh fruits. In front of the boys was what they could only describe as heaven; a lengthy table covered in platters of all kinds of food.

Neither of them stopped themselves from rushing to the table, and picking up fistfuls of sapid steak covered in hot gravy and candied oranges. Leo chuckled in delight as sweet juices from the fruit dribbled down his chin, and River smiled widely at this. He then ripped off a large piece of bread from one of the plates, and shoved it in his mouth. This made Leo giggle more, and eventually both boys were nearly howling in laughter.

"Hey! What in the world do you think you're doing?!" yelled a short, chubby man as he stomped towards the pair. His face was red, and his veins were popping out. Both River and Leo stopped instantly, and River spotted a black door out of the corner of his eye. He stuffed handfuls of food into his pockets, then swiftly grabbed his friend by his arm, and they both bolted towards the door.

It was all a blur for River. He and Leo ran out the door, and kept running with the vexed man chasing and yelling curses at them. He kept running until his feet felt like lead and his lungs were on fire. That was when he realized, he couldn't hear the man anymore and he wasn't holding Leo's arm. Oh no.

Rivers' head snapped in every direction, his eyes desperately scanning the place for his best friend. He walked around a nearby corner and saw two glass doors on the opposite wall. Through the glass, the boy could see a vast garden and gate leading to a road. This was it. He thought.

This was how he could get out.

River felt the mounds of food in his pockets. He could leave now and forget about everything. He'd find another mansion somewhere, and beg for some money. Surely someone had some cash to spare. However, just as he was about to open the door, he remembered his life with Leo. He remembered when they played together many years ago, and how they never failed to make each other laugh. Escaping wasn't worth it. Not without Leo. Then, River found himself racing back and looking for Leo. After a few minutes, he saw two moving figures through a gap between two doors. Opening them and walking through, River could see the man grab Leo's shaking figure.

"Wait!" River cried out, his voice raspy and panting.

"Please, let us go. We were just trying to find some food. It's been so long since we've had our last meal."

The man paused, and a look of sympathy flashed over his face as he noticed Leo's hollow cheeks and scrawny figure. "If anyone finds out I let you escape, I'd be dead in seconds," he replied.

"We won't tell anyone. We promise," Leo said timidly.

"Well then, how would I explain the mess in the kitchen?"

"Rats?" River piped up, giving the man a pleading look.

Said man stood there for a while, his eyebrows knitting together in thought. He then let go of Leo's collar and nodded at River. "Go, and do it quickly. The front doors are across the landing and around the corner."

"Thank you, sir," they muttered simultaneously whilst walking out of the room.

"You could've left me, you know. I'm pretty sure it wouldn't have taken long for you to get out of here," Leo stated, breaking the uncomfortable silence.

"I know, but I would never leave you alone, Leo," River started, "you're all I've got. Plus, I need you just as much as you need me. We're best friends, and best friends stay together."

Lan'ia

by George Bou Habib

"Look! Look down there!" His voice could just about be heard above the sound of the aeroplane's engine and the shrieking wind in their ears. "Can you see it?" exclaimed Noah.

"Yep! Crystal clear," replied Adam.

They could barely hear each other over the deafening sounds around them, but what they could see stunned them. In awe, they gazed, at its gracefulness, its speed, how it flapped its captivating wings.

They thought to themselves, 'What a majestic creature,' this was truly something else. It wasn't a bird, it was an angel!

Without any sign, it began approaching the boys, who were in a trance, and it beckoned them to hop on. Without hesitation, the two youngsters hopped on the bird. They felt a feeling they have never felt before. They fell into a sensation of tranquility, it was like a dream. However, a moment of realization hit the boys, where are we going? Where is this bird taking us? The airplane could no longer be seen.

'Uh oh,' Noah thought to himself. I didn't look they would be returning home anytime soon. Nevertheless, Adam didn't have a care in the world; he was ecstatic! As they sat back and cherish the ride, they noticed the bird beginning to make its descent. As the clouds cleared up and the sun shine bright in their eyes, they began to look around, scanning for where they might land.

"Look!" screeched Adam.

They both looked at the beauty before them,

it was an island what seemed to be the shape of three large, connected rings, it looked so magnificent it made the boys feel euphoric!

As they approached the island, a breezy of tropic aromas mixed with strong, fresh air hit them. "Ahhh," Adam let out a breath of relief.

The boys disembarked the bird as it touched the ground. As they dusted themselves after the heck of a ride, they noticed footsteps approaching them. Noah, who was tying laces gazed up and gestured Adam to do the same.

They were taller than the average human, their skin amethyst purple, with lizard green eyes, their hair all slicked back they wore leaves and animal skin on them. What was about to occur could either end well, or go horribly wrong. The leader of the group stepped forward, he was the biggest most dominant of the pack.

He declared, "Who are these people and who has brought them here?"

The two boys looked around for the bird, but it was nowhere to be seen. "Uh, um, t- t-the bb-bird sir," stuttered Adam.

"Hmm, and you two are?"

"N-noah and uh Ad-dam," murmured the boys in unison.

"Well, my name is Sa A'kur, I am the leader of the Lan'ian tribe, this is my family, where do you boys come from?"

The boys tension began to come to an ease, "The UAE!" blurted out Adam.

A look of confusion appeared on the Lan'ians faces, and whispers of uncertainty were heard in the now crowd that had gathered around the boys.

"Where is this?" inquired Sa A'kur.

"On earth?" replied Noah.

A look of realization and panic became visible on the tribes faces and everybody took a step back, the feeling of unease returned to the boys as a voice shouted, "Get rid of these evil souls on our land, they come from the wicked land of earth!"

However, Sa A'kur remained calm and replied, "They are only children, what harm could they bring to us?"

He approached them and pointed out, "You boys have entered a portal which led to our Galaxy, The Neximus way, to Our planet, Shi N'aa and to our country, Lan'ia".

The boys realized they were too busy enjoying the ride on the bird they didn't even notice their passing through this so called portal!

"Please, don't hurt us, we didn't mean anything!" shouted Adam.

Sa A'kur comforted them. "Everything will be

okay, you shall remain with us for now, in the humble land of Lan'ia, until we find out how to return you to earth, this is Sili, my daughter, she will stay with you and show you around, if anything is needed from me, just tell Sili, and I shall be there."

The crowd began to fade, as everyone returned to what they were doing.

As he was just leaving, Adam told Sa A'kur, "Thank you, Sir."

"Please, call me A'kur, everyone does," Adam grinned.

"Come on! Follow me!" exclaimed Sili. "I shall introduce you to the kids of L'ania, we are a small tribe, but one filled with love and joy, we shall teach you to swim with the sea birds, how to hunt for food, and so much more!"

That sounded great to the boys, but after a long day, they needed some rest.

"Of course, I shall lead you to your hut. As they walked to the hut, Sili pointed out everything that the boys should know before staying here.

"Us kids don't really have much work to do, just make sure your hut is clean, whereas the adults of Lan'ia have to hunt for food, make us clothes, bathe the animals, build new huts and lots of other things; when we turn fifteen, all of this becomes our duty!"

After ten minutes, they arrived to the hut, "Now, I will be in the hut next to you, so if you need anything, just knock on my door!" said Sili as she exited the boys hut and shut the door.

It was 9:58, The boys shut off the lights, rested their heads on the pillows and by 10:00 they were fast asleep.

"Good morning boys! Wake up, it's time to swim and ride the winged-fish!" Shining bright light hit the boys eyes as Sili opened the curtains.

"Let me sleep," groaned Noah, however Adam was already up and about.

"Yay! I can't wait to swim with the fish!" The boys got dressed, however this time in traditional Lan'ian clothes, they wore fur skin and large leaves. As Sili took them to the shore to see the winged fish, their heart began to race; they were huge!

"How are we supposed to ride these beasts?" said Noah.

"Don't worry, they are the friendliest!" exclaimed a voice. It wasn't Sili, so who would it be?

"Ahh, I forgot to introduce you, these are my friends, Ikaari, Uulia and Ohoney," Sili started, "Ikaari and Uulia are siblings, and O'huney's mother is soon to have another child! You will see them around a lot!"

The boys began to swim, along with their new friends and they even rode the winged fish! It was an experience of a lifetime for them, yet little did the boys know what was awaiting them.

The sun was setting, the group of friends were heading to the huts, laughing, talking about the highlights of their day, and what they would do tomorrow, then suddenly three, tall, mid-teenage boys walked towards them, they stopped them in their tracks, and began talking.

"You two boys are not welcome here. You must leave. Now."

"No! They are our friends, and unless you want to mess with us, you shall mess with my father, the Sa A'kur," said Sili.

"Hahahaha!" the boys laughed, "you better watch out, cause we'll be back."

They left as they muttered and whispered, "Don't worry about them, they can't do anything to you," said O'huney.

"Yeah, honestly don't listen to them," added Uulia.

"Those were Kaeah, Xenimah and Re'sam, the most disliked boys on Lan'ia," said Akur.

As Sili told her father, "You must keep a very close eye on the boys hut tonight, and if anything, absolutely anything happens, you ring the emergency bell."

"Yes father, I will be sure of this."

Later that night, the boys were getting ready for bed, they talked about how this all happened so fast, "Well, I am not mad about it, we are having the best time," said Adam.

"Well, I guess so, goodnight," replied Noah.

12:00, the boys were fast asleep. It was thought that everyone on Lan'ia was fast asleep, however Kaeah, Xenimah and Re'sam had snuck into the boys's hut. Together, the evil Lan'ians kidnapped Noah and Adam even before Sili could get to them. They tied them up to a post outside. Slowly, Adam's eyes began to open and he was met with pure darkness. As he got his bearings, he noticed that he was not longer asleep in his given bed. He was tied up. Next to him, was Noah who was regaining consciousness. They began to hear voices...

"What do we do with them?" "I suppose we ship them back home? How about into space? Kaeah suggested. But then a bellowing voice was heard, and multiple footsteps "ENOUGH NOW, OR ELSE THE CONSEQUENCES WILL BE EXCEEDINGLY UNPLEASANT!"

"It's A'kur!" squealed Noah and Adam in a syncopated tone! Now, the boys knew, knew that that they would be safe and sound.

Printed in Great Britain
by Amazon

25104908R00136